Life beckons.

Sometimes it whispers. Sometimes it sings. Occasionally it screams.

Life had always conversed with Madison Peacock. She had heard it, but hadn't always listened. After the sudden death of her mother in 1995, Madison had gotten used to ignoring life and only hearing raging chaos. She had run far and away from her family and charged straight into a train wreck with her first husband, Rhett Peacock. Before his ambiguous death in 2007, Rhett had taken Madison down deep into his dark, turbulent life.

Choices. Life whispers, sings, or screams choices.

The choice to leave her husband, Houston King, was the catalyst. Madison would finally follow her heart, build her life with Dyer Brown. Houston was packed and ready to leave. Instead he died. The blatant irony. Her not-so-perfect new life on the gulf beach upended with raging symmetry she could no longer ignore. Madison Peacock's life was now screaming in alarming pitches. Death the theme.

This death pulled in the close acquaintances surrounding her old, disastrous life back in Little Rock. Madison's estranged Aunt M reappeared, opening doors Madison had slammed shut with her mother's death. Gabrielle Vansant, her beach neighbor, soon became that unintended ally. The very people from Madison's past that she had refuted were the connections most important in the cosmic justice her life doled. Madison's past tragedies would turn out to be the greatest gifts in eradicating the anarchy surrounding her.

Whether Madison listened or not *now* was her most important choice.

Everywhere

and

Nowhere

Monica C. Petter

First published by Monica C. Petter

ISNB: 978-0-578-22668-2

First Printed by Instantpublisher.com

Cover Art © Monica C. Petter

We are all artists and art, creating our lives with our choices, shaped by our circumstances that in turn create our faces.

~Monica C. Petter

This book is dedicated in memory of my
mother, Mary Ann.
Hearts to you, mom.

October 2014

Death of Hubris

October on the beach was still warm, humid. The promise of change was always noted in the fragrant scents from new winds that blew into the gulf. Tourists began their sojourns south to this peaceful homage to summer memories. Those who lived on this beach grasped mornings and evenings as gifts or perks of their residence.

The Monday morning rush was typical for Madison's household. Most Mondays. Today was somber as low tide. Hannah was preteen moody and quiet. Peck was rambunctious and loud as they made their lunches for school. Hannah kept looking around the room suspiciously and particularly in the corner where suitcases had metastasized overnight. Peck was just five-year-old oblivion, lost in his own ninja world. He hadn't noticed his mom's swollen, red eyes as Hannah had. Girls, women feel each others' emotions whether they understand them or not.

Madison hurried the kids as their ride's horn blew in the drive. Madison kissed Peck on the cheek and wiped the jelly off his chin as he wiggled to the door.

"Where is Houston?" Hannah shot a stare to the suitcases.

"He's running." Madison studied her daughter's pursed lips.

"He's leaving, isn't he...for good?" Madison brushed her long blond hair over her ear and they smiled through shared tears.

"Yes." Words made it real. Hannah hugged her mother.

Hubris is defined as excessive pride or self-confidence. It can be human nature when one thinks they are in control of every situation. Hubris clung to every nook and cranny Houston King touched. He was a savior and wore that label like a Rolex. Like a dropped sack of flour, it kept showing up in inappropriate places no matter how hard he tried to wash it away. It was what he knew.

It was labeled with love, but the motivation was fear.

Madison had just gotten dressed and noticed that Houston had not returned from his morning beach run. She had hoped he would get his bags as she showered and slip off into his own life once again. The hard things had been spoken the evening before. Madison assumed with this delay that Houston was not going to make this exit easy. His fear had an odd bravado that always made Madison stay. As she gathered her purse, a loud pounding on the door made her drop everything. Madison greeted the emphatic thumps to find her neighbor, Lowe Vandeven. An instinct from Madison's past life rippled familiar panic that moved in a wave. Lowe had found Houston face down in the sand. Houston was gone alright. Dead on the beach. Lowe had called 911 and they had arrived and confirmed Houston King had a massive heart attack that killed him instantly. Even hubris was mortal. As Lowe held Madison close to her in consolation, she spied the masculine suitcases in the room that practically unzipped themselves and spoke. Lowe's family had lived a gyspy existence. Like bread and water, suitcases were staples in her home.

Lowe had spent many evenings babysitting Peck and Hannah. Madison's patio healing comfort. When Lowe and Madison had first locked eyes this Monday, there was something more purposeful. Lowe was instantly akin. She stayed near as an empathetic anchor. Madison made the dreaded call to Houston's only family, his daughter who lived in Dallas. Madison had been on the receiving end of that grim reaper moment, had known how to bury a rotten husband with precision. Houston and his daughter didn't jive. Angry sobs ended the conversation abruptly. Madison paced a three-foot rectangle back and forth. Somehow the heavens override our rational minds in moments of crisis and death. Harshness gets muffled and the spirits that guide our lives rub us on the back with warm consolation. Life was playing out in frenetic slow motion. A heavenly host of deceased voices rushed her ears in unison. Madison's wheels began flying off of her disciplined machine. She called Dyer.

Dyer picked up Hannah and Peck from school and rushed to Madison. Lowe opened the door to Dyer and the kids as a catatonic Madison sat on the couch, staring at Houston's suitcases. Peck was an energy bomb, headed toward his newly dead father's neatly packed belongings. Dyer snatched his arm, holding him close to his side. Hannah rhythmically sobbed, hiding her shameful cheer from earlier in the day behind her delicate fingers that covered her mouth and nose. Everyone stared at Houston's suitcases. Lowe took unaware Peck outside as she felt warm tears blur her vision. The energy bordered macabre. Lowe had only known shallow roots since birth. Walking upon a dead man established roots in something much more. Dyer, Madison, and

Hannah all embraced in a circle around the luggage with mortified sentiment that ran much deeper than sorrow.

Rusting

I lost me
Orphaned my past
Cherry picked memories
For the fast.

An adequate shell
A hollow core
An empty canvas
An open door.

That open wound
Without a suture
Bleeding my past, my present
And my future.

A haggard savant
I began to teach.
I've got promise
I've got reach.

Only when
I began to disappear
Did I rust until
I had no fear

And So It Begins

Time was never guaranteed. Sudden absence and loss reassured those mindful that depth and breadth of living truly was the purpose of moving our feet. A long, happy life was a manmade concept. The best lives are difficult. The concept that we start in diapers and end in diapers isn't appealing to most. Houston in particular. He had packed more living into his sixty something frame. His life was full of the real everyday drama. The sort of strife parents shields their children from, manifesting their own fears onto their offspring, molding their character. It was apropos that Houston died from a heart attack. He had such heart and it tried to best his ego. Houston had been a man with a lot of power. He used it for good; yet he was human, tried to create protection for all he loved. In his early adulthood, it ended up making him miserable. He had gotten better with each relationship, especially the one with Madison.

Instead of holding her so tightly, he let her go. And then he died. His learning complete.

Death was messy. Funerals seemed Madison's second career. She had buried both her parents and her first husband. She understood as a counselor that each death got easier to plan, but much harder to compartmentalize. It robbed that rooted control she had mastered with weird ticks and oddities. Tears now rained phantom as rage. Catatonia balanced the two. She sat staring at Houston's suitcases in brief spurts often replaying their conversation from the night before. It made complete sense in hindsight, yet it pissed her off, caught her off guard. Wedges pinched. Madison had known Houston and his daughter had a complicated relationship. Trust had been scarce between the two. So, Houston had put Madison as the executor of his estate, the impartial voice. Houston hadn't realized that he had placed Madison in the same position she had been assigned in her other, despicable life. That choice would upend her and send her careening.

Houston's daughter had arrived late in the evening. Madison had welcomed his daughter and let her stay in her father's home. Lowe had taken Hannah and Peck to stay next door for the evening. Madison hadn't tided up the corners neatly. She gave up total control; the fair and precise thing to do and let Houston's family make the funeral arrangements. Then, she bolted. Death was driving that wedge between who Madison thought she was and who she was meant to become.

Safe Places

Dyer was standing on the steps to his deck, texting Hannah good night, when he felt Madison wrap her arms around his waist. There was artful precision as she crept into the corners of his periphery, unaware. He turned into her embrace. She was trembling in mighty bursts she couldn't reel in.

"I can't do this anymore." Madison's voice fell hush to her agony. Dyer just pulled her head close to his shoulder as he had done Hannah when she was feeling wounded.

"I just walked away...I can't breathe that air." Dyer felt her warm tears as she nestled the nape of his neck, tickling it with her words.

"What can I do for you?" Dyer stroked her hair with his stumpy fingers that were clumsy but kind.

"Just let me stay." Madison held him tighter.

They clasped hands as Dyer walked her inside his simple home. She loved how it smelled of lumber and leather. It was her safe place.

"I'll be right back." He disappeared into his bedroom.

She heard the faucet engage. The cadence of water off the old claw foot tub sang to her soul. Dyer just watched her from his bedroom doorway as she found his whiskey and poured them a glass.

She met him in the doorway, their faces studying the other. He just liked the way she occupied a space.

"To old times." Madison raised her glass.

"Come on…you know you want to do it." Dyer grinned as Madison downed the whiskey then threw the plastic glass into the wall where it bounced off ineffectively. He wished the old fashioned glass had been crystal for her sake.

"Good enough." She wiped her mouth and closed her eyes, exhaling in a loud wave.

Dyer eyed the bath and she moved in the direction of his manly soap. Madison wrote their love song with her gaze as she shut the bathroom door. Dyer swam in Madison's blue-eyed sorrow.

She emerged from the bathroom wrapped in a towel, her hair a wet wavy mass that bloomed spicy shampoo. She opened the drawer that had her things in it. The drawer that she often used when she snuck away from that air in Houston's beach house. It had been freshly stocked earlier in the week as she prepared that freedom conversation with Houston. Just in case things went south, she'd have a place to run. Run she had.

A shared history between Dyer and Madison had created home no matter the proximity. Shared space, shared history always begot love. Dyer was sitting on the glider couch on the screened-in porch, listening to the waves fight and roar. The tides were bully and brute in the darkness, pushing the sand hard into the shore. The screen door creaked as Madison joined him. The salt air humid, but not suffocating. Hints of fall. He reached for her hand. They sat for a long while in silence. The energy was kinetic. She was sitting exactly where she had intended to be that morning, but now under deeper, darker circumstances.

Madison begun to cry again. Fitful stops and starts, the guilt salted her tears. She put her face in her weakened hands. Dyer found his own tears pooling in the lines around his eyes. He knew Madison was shifting like the beaten sand and it scared him. He wanted to catch all the pieces of her and put them back together, knowing it was impossible.

"Kiss me." A simple gesture laced with intimacy grounded the lost. Dyer opened his mouth to hers, inviting her below the safety of the physical. The kiss was slow, reminiscent. Madison grunted and sniveled, succumbing to the warm affection Dyer breathed into her.

"Thank you…" Madison face was flushed, a shy girl. She nuzzled into Dyer's stubbly cheeks, consoled. To know someone's core was a gift. To trust enough to drop walls was communion.

Dyer enveloped Madison and they gave the anguish to the night. The horrible day collapsed to the space between their beating hearts. They postured face to face and fell horizontal into the swing of the glider. Their breathing synced as they fell asleep. The tides suddenly withdrew their fists and began a rhythmic lullaby.

Dyer Brown

Build solid foundations for those you believe in. I learned that lesson the hard way. I didn't believe in much when I was younger. My parents never practiced what they preached so their words never hit home. I married the first girl who paid attention to me. I think she loved what I could be. I wasn't patient or understanding with her. We adopted Hannah, but I was still not happy. When she died suddenly, it made me an angry, selfish man. It turned me into all the bad versions of myself. I held onto the old, cracking foundations even though. I didn't trust in what I had built. My house fell.

Death bonds people. Madison was a woman that scared me with logic I respected. She shared so much of herself with me in the cross roads of our lives. We were in a strange relationship, our own world. There was nothing pretend or brave. It was simple, everyday kind of stuff. The stuff of family. The real crap that scared us both. Even more than Madison's very complex past. It was much more real than we would admit. I love Madison in deep ways I never could with anyone else. We connected and it broke everything I had known about rules. It was about trusting in the right gut things. I was building a foundation with a woman who taught me how to trust. A woman I couldn't own. One that loves for all the right reasons. That opened my eyes.

Houston King was another thing. He was a man with a lot of power and money. When the ones you love are in danger, power is good to have on your side. Houston was on Madison's side. He saved her from her old life and helped her build a new one – with him. The old me would have walked away from Madison. A prideful man has a hard time even thinking about letting go of control, much less handing his woman over to another. I was angry and hurt. But, it was her choice. I had strong-armed Madison in the past. I pulled and she pushed back hard. I was a very, stupid man once. Something more I couldn't explain had taken over. I knew I was not going backwards or be that selfish again. It only pushed the people I loved away. I'd let Houston be that prideful ass. In the end, money and power couldn't buy Madison. She was never for sale.

Houston and Madison had finally agreed to go their separate ways. They say the third time is a charm. I've waited for Madison. Houston packed his bags and just suddenly died. This type of death changed everything. Even the air. This is sending Madison far into her past. She is cracking. At least I caught her. I've paid her back for all those years ago when she saved me and Hannah. Now we are even. The foundation we built long ago is stronger. Our home will get built. Madison is part of me no matter the situation.

M is for Mirror

A gentle, cleansing thundershower and the smell of French toast brought Dyer and Madison back to the new morning. They were now in Dyer's bed, snuggled safely in his sheets that smelled of their mingled skin. Dyer had awakened shortly after midnight as Hannah was sneaking back into his house. She would be a terrible burglar, her footsteps leaded. Hannah had found them asleep on the swing outside, kissed her mother's cheek. Her tears rained on Madison's unaware brow and temple. Dyer moved he and Madison back into the house, back into his bed. Madison sleep cried most of the evening. Dyer just held her in those moments. She would whimper and sob like a dog barking in its sleep, oddly audible. Other times she'd moan a very weary tirade in a language he knew too well.

Dyer was showering when he smelled the French toast. Hannah was surprising them with breakfast. She loved pampering. He was tucking his shirt in when the bedroom door slowly navigated open. Hannah peered around the door frame, a periscope, one blue eye and strand of long, blonde hair searching for parents. Dyer winked at her. She offered breakfast on an old tray he had fashioned out of a wooden box top. She set the tray on the nightstand and curled up beside her sleeping mother on the bed. Mothers and daughters sense proximity. Hannah kissed her mother's neck and Madison opened her eyes, turning to her daughter, kissing her square on the mouth.

"Morning Momma. I love you." Hannah's cheer was sunshine through the showers.

"Oh, my Hannah Beth. I'm sorry about all this." Hannah loved how her mother apologized for people's misgivings. Especially the dead ones.

"I'm just glad you are here… with us." Hannah took a bite of the French toast. She fed Madison a bite. She offered some to Dyer who stood in the corner, admiring a view similar to one so many years ago. A private place, a memory in all their minds that only changed with older versions of themselves.

Dyer and Hannah had gone to check on Peck. Madison made the hard phone calls. Houston's daughter confirmed she was taking him back to Dallas and burying him next to her mother. In life, Houston would have hated that idea, had run from that life he was ashamed of on personal levels. In death, Madison knew he'd want his daughter to be a part of honoring his life.

The showers had matched the mood, somber and quiet. The everyday hum had been replaced with a deafening silence. It was heavy and so intense it moved everyone's feet. Madison had just finished her phone calls when there was a rapping on Dyer's door. It was a persistent, white knuckle knock that meant business. Madison released the knob with evident irritation when an older version of her mother met her gaze. A salt and pepper mop-headed woman with clear blue eyes startled Madison. Her eyes plumbed to

Madison's soul that sent her stomach to her toenails. Her frame was slight but her presence mighty. There was a sincere authority about her that sidled people. Honesty that shed truths in all she said.

"What are you doing here, M?" Madison was a bit afraid of her Aunt Mirabella.

"Houston's dead." M spoke as if Madison needed the confirmation, pushing her way inside her life.

"Who told you?" Madison's temples throbbed as her life ambushed and betrayed her symmetry.

"He did." M kissed Madison on the cheek. Madison's anger turned wet and snotty again.

"Don't do that to me." Madison and M had shared a long, strained synergy. Madison felt M's small arms wrap around her and cradle her much taller frame with motherly gusto. This was a long overdue olive branch.

"Don't you be so afraid, dearest." Madison could almost hear her mother's echo in M's pitch.

"I'm glad you are here...whatever voodoo you hear." Madison chirped lightheartedly, but she knew her aunt had misunderstood, beautiful gifts of timing.

"Portent was the word he whispered – it means omen or warning." M stroked Madison's bobbed hair, hair she used to brush one hundred times before putting up into a pony tail as a child.

"He was right." Madison sighed. M left the how and why for other times.

Madison and M had weathered many a momentous calamity together. These women, fashioned from the same cloth, found solace in their like fabric. Madison needed someone with a firm constitution since her own nature had left her incessantly hurdling each obstacle. M saw her sister, Marcella, in Madison and had known how to manage her sister's daring. This unlikely duo bore shallow roots. Both had scathed enough death that it uprooted their feet.

Dyer trounced their reunion, sporting a razor dry grin. Dyer and M shared an understanding that played out like a poker hand. He wrapped around Madison very protectively. M felt the barbed wire he wrapped subtly around the world he and Madison fostered. She envied the ardor he wore like a sheriff's pointed star. Dyer had been an elemental key in eradicating Madison's disasters rather than complicating them. He was part of the good.

Mirabella Shireman

Early as my first memories I knew I was different. I knew things. I didn't know how I knew these things, they just were. I had parents that were middle-classed hard working people. They had no special knowledge or higher cognition that they passed on to me. They just loved me and taught by example. When adults thought me just a child, I reasoned the heavy, unspoken. I had empathy that ran deep into a space I didn't tap into, but rather, tapped into me. I was never afraid of that kind of trust. It felt natural as love, so I listened. As I got older, the world called me into the hum of society – manmade sort of logistics that didn't always feel just. I straddled both places, wanting to blend in with the people I was surrounded by, yet feeling very squeezed and uncomfortable. The world said I was to be one way, as if who I was intended to be was wrong. This sort of being led me to my true self. Man's fears dubbed the unique as strange.

I had an older sister, Marcella. She was five years my senior and ruled the sibling turf with love and adventure. My sister and I were consummate sleuths. Both our parents worked, so we entertained ourselves outside in lands we created. We acted out Agatha Christie novels in our own backyards, surmising the usual suspects, yet finding the perpetrator cleverly cloaked in plain sight. I suppose it made sense that both of us would go into law enforcement. Marcella was fiery and bull-headed and I was more rational and thought provoked with connectedness I minimized. My gift of knowing helped me focus better than most. Marcella excelled as a detective, but secretly loved the rush of the everyday chase. I wanted to be just a detective.

In law enforcement, there were many unspoken givens. There was a very definite line between good and evil when working with facts. Gray areas fingered the ill-intended. Private life was your true face and work life was laced with inconsistency, no repeated routine. It kept you safe and on point. Good cops don't make predictable pattern waves. They rippled infrequently. Marcella and I rippled better than most. We especially kept our private lives a mystery.

Marcella was killed suddenly and with great purpose. Someone was playing chicken, hugging center line. Marcella manned her side of a challenge, her favorite pulse of valor. She gave in first and swerved erratically, causing a chain reaction that sent us end over end. Marcella died instantly. It was deemed a horrible tragedy, but my knowing told me differently. In those flashes after the crash, I recalled things I shouldn't, that no one would freely share, just know. I kept that stuff close to me. From that day, I moved through the world with heightened brows. I did a lot of hand-holding with fearlessness. I rippled, a master gypsy. My career path shifted. I began to help people get justice with these new skills. Justice mattered, not by means, but the intention.

Bad things happened for good reasons. Those new to grief fight it with a grounded ego. Lesson only wasted if they fell upon deaf ears. Madison had that thrill of the chase like her mother. Marcella tried to warn Madison of this sort of fast car. Her death sped Madison faster, right into her first husband's manipulative arms. That engine miserably burned out. But when Houston died, I knew Madison's ego would be dust. Madison and I grew in awkward directions, but fate always lead our footsteps along the same crooked path. When I made the decision to go to Madison, I recognized portentous change was intended for me just as much.

January 1995 - The Incidentals

The ordinary, the mundane rush of a Tuesday was upon the busy highway. The traffic was a slower go with remnants of ice and snow from Sunday night's winter surprise. Little Rock drivers weren't used to the winter weather and always drove like crazy teenagers that had let their yet developed frontal lobes man the wheel. Today was no exception as fender benders and side-ways cars dotted the main roadways into the metro.

Marcella cursed the crawl as she pumped the breaks in a rhythm that matched the thumping motor of her police car. Mirabella watched her sister from the passenger side. Marcella had road rage as she squirmed, a worm in hot ash. The exit, merely half a mile away, was a proverbial carrot on a string that egged her impatience.

"This is like, what – the fifth bumper you've replaced? Don't even think about it, Marcella. Be patient." M saw her sister mentally navigating the aloof driver in front of her. She was not going to listen. Bumper six was a go.

"Oh, shut it, M." Marcella pumped the brakes, hit the gas, and swerved around the car in front of her. They scathed bumpers by inches and barreled down the easement to the exit she had been anticipating. This was an alternate route that most found out of the way. Marcella liked it because there was little traffic.

"What's with the nasty disposition?" M felt the sudden maneuver was like a bullet from a gun, totally intended for someone other than the innocent driver.

"I got to meet Madison's boyfriend, Rhett. Total douche bag." Marcella didn't mince her feelings. She didn't elaborate either.

"That's charming. What did he do to you?" M threw out the bait and just reeled her sister in slowly.

"I don't like his super white fake teeth and expensive clothes. They hide things. Things I don't want my daughter to unearth." Marcella spoke through clenched teeth.

"So she's smitten by his command and power…hmmm…like mother like daughter. You'd better tread lightly. I know how you react if someone dislikes the ones you love." Mirabella had never witnessed such blatant dislike of Madison's choice in men until now.

"Whatever. He's bad news like I've never felt. There's a shift happening and I don't like it, sister." Marcella's mouth turned down in true fear.

"Did you tell Madison?" M saw her sister grip the steering wheel harder.

"I tried. She totally cut me off." Marcella noticed fog patches in the distance.

"Marcella, she'll have to figure this one out on her own. She's a smart lady." M understood her sister's protectiveness. Madison was her only child.

"She is so smart, but her heart isn't, but that is not what scares me. I sense we are all in for some shit hitting the fan." Marcella's motherly fears swelled in her erratic speed.

An oncoming motorist in the distance passed into the center lane. Those seconds hoping the car would return felt like minutes of time. A choice had to be made. M saw her sister frozen in indecision. They were going to lose more than a bumper.

"Swerve!" M belted it out with labored lungs. She had been holding her breath. Marcella swerved and they careened into a foggy pasture, flipping end over end. The other car managed to regain control.

On the cold, desolate country highway, the only sound heard was the car cracking and popping as the wheels spun, sluggishly winding down on the police car. M wasn't hearing with her ears any longer. It was a hum of world energy she began to sense. Her vision was above the car, floating in the fog like a bird on weightless wings that hovers and searches. There was no sense of gravity, just vivid insight. Everything around her was a rainbow of light as she seemed to ascend like a jet into the low hum. Familiar voices from her past bled out in the low hum she felt. They communicated one after the other now, offering love and comfort. Marcella pierced the chatter with brevity and command.

"YOU have to take care of Madison for me. You're her mirror now." Marcella's boom of energy and surety had fervently bested the others.

And like that, M fell heavy as a lead balloon and she began to feel pushed back into narrowness. In her descent, she saw the car that had caused the split second decision to veer right. It was pulled over as a young woman in her twenties checked a crying toddler in a car seat. The woman raced across the road to the upside down police car. M felt crushing, labored breaths move through her broken body as she opened her eyes slightly to the young woman staring at her through a cracked and half-broken windshield. As M was losing consciousness again, the young woman calmly uttered *I'll get help.*

The young woman who went for help was Gabby. Gabby had been riding in the car with Rhett, who swerved as she checked her young baby girl in the backseat, conveniently killing the last stronghold to getting Madison, inadvertently linking Gabby with her birth mother. Yet, they were all tethered in life through their associations with Rhett Peacock. They all lost and gained family that day.

M woke up a month later from a medically induced coma in a Little Rock hospital to find that her sister had been killed in the crash. Madison had buried and tidied up her mother's small life into a small storage bin. The crash was chalked up to the weather and the police report noted Marcella had over corrected by the tire and skid marks on the highway. M's memory of that crash was fragmented and repressed somewhere deep in her guarded psyche. Madison grew distant from her aunt, who only made her miss her own mother and seethe over the circumstances. There was no love lost, but none shared between them either. Death had such swift power that Madison coped by drawing closer to the toxic boyfriend with all the power she needed. Eventually, Madison married Rhett Peacock and fueled her anger toward the loss of her mother. She dared death with his shady business dealings. M was now alone. She had lost her best friend, her sister, and her only family, Madison. She recovered her broken body, but her spirit was forever changed. M and Madison both moved through their worlds differently. Marcella, the very person that bonded them in life, now challenged them to change with her death.

Forward

Tears were like oxygen. They opened the soul with a release of cosmic baggage. Madison had not cried so much in her entire life. Not for nothing or no one and especially not herself. Once the waves had begun, they crashed like a tsunami, with a fit of fury and momentum that couldn't be reeled in or damned. The pain, the anger, the betrayal and sense of loneliness exited her physical shell like bats from a belfry. The strange moodiness, the walls crumbled and all that was left was the fragile, rich woman Madison had left frozen in time. A new set of wisdom clothed her like new skin. Madison could no longer deny the things left undone.

Dyer knew M was bringing the kids back soon. He could see Madison's mental gymnastics and knew she planned to really open up to her aunt. He saw Madison's fear of walking with this vulnerable, fragile newness. Madison rounded the corner and there was something in the whites of her eyes that was fresh, new. He couldn't put his finger on it. Her eyes were different. They looked upon him kinder, more knowing, fearless in honest ways. Madison kissed Dyer on the cheek and in their stare lay hints of their broken past that would always glimmer slightly. But there was a finality to some of the puppeteers of her past. Their connection was sidelined with a few quick knocks on the door as Hannah peered around the frame, telescoping the room with her big blue eyeball. She noticed the collusion on her parents' shared grin. Something was up. Peck pushed her through the door as he wormed around his gangly taller sister. He crash landed into the center of Madison and Dyer's united front. Peck was always direct and to the point in his honest intentions. Hannah hesitated, holding onto the doorknob. M pushed the door open and Hannah conceded to her

parents' side. There was a grace in the way M
moved through a space. She seemed to be the
security blanket on any heated situation. Everyone
shared a smile and the family gears shifted
forward.

Truths and Anniversaries

Choices painted a life. Some choices
followed a life like a shadow, defining and
reminding with brevity. Some choices expedited
the inevitable. Life has a predetermined path
unknown to the one walking it. Everyone's life
was connected to another, flowing into each other,
a mod ballet. Every step important to each
involved, a team endeavor completed only when
all participated. Death didn't exclude one from the
dance, but rather enhanced the steps.

M watched Madison prepare their lunch.
She cut their sandwiches just like Marcella,
diagonally and with a similar fastidiousness.
Sharing the same space wearied their bodies as if

they were wearing wet blankets of unsaid on their shoulders. Madison placed the sandwiches on the table, shields of sorts between women. Food a peacekeeper.

"So, it's been twenty years." Madison exhaled as she said it as if the air had been trapped around the words.

"What do you want to tell me, Madison?" M knew the details of that day floated in a cloud above them just waiting to sing.

"I guess my unspoken truth." Madison's eyes wept through her smile.

"You have the right to your feelings. She was your mother. I am sorry you had to handle everything." M smiled slightly.

"I just hate that our last words were angry ones. I didn't mind handling her things. I didn't handle you, I ran. I am sorry I left you alone. I left me, too." Madison heard the ice shift with force in her iced tea glass. Both women's eyes gravitated to the glass with a smile.

"I heard you, Mom. She is always on point." Madison and M chuckled softly, lost in their own memories.

"You still dreaming about your mom?" M broached the sticky subject. Madison wasn't as receptive to those sorts of untethered spaces. She liked to be firmly planted as her mother taught her.

"Like mad since Houston died." Tears rained a beautiful waterfall of grief. M reached across the plates and found Madison's fingers.

"You've got to start opening all those little boxes you put everyone you lost into along with your enormous grief. Trust me. They will find you eventually." M sensed other heartbeats in their perimeter.

"She was so vivid this last time. We were doing something normal together like always and she told me she missed me." The long, dry lines around Madison's eyes were finally moist, giving her a youthful suppleness.

"She didn't like your first choice of a husband. That was virtually our last conversation. She swerved and met an oncoming car and that was it… Someone reported the accident." M's radar was now more heightened to the other heartbeats.

The wall seemed to be imbibing their conversation a bit too closely. She used her covert senses to case the room and surrounding windows. Madison noticed her pique.

"So, the police report was just speculation from an eyewitness – neatly tucked away?" Madison connected the dots.

"I didn't remember much for a long, long time…but yes, I didn't challenge it. I didn't tell you back then, but I suspected it wasn't just an accident." Madison could sense a protective barrier of kindness M walled around the uncomfortable.

"What's going on?" Madison used her crocodile gaze as she cased her periphery. Both women were attuned to something more.

"I'm not quite sure…but we are being heard." M winked at Madison just as she had her own sister – a silent affirmation of investigation.

M cleared the plates from the table and began putting them in the dishwasher. Madison wiped tears as she joined her in the kitchen. Both assessed their surroundings with different abilities. As M placed the final dish into the dishwasher, M and Madison noticed a shadow bob out of sight in the neighbor's upstairs window. Madison gulped all the air she could swallow.

"Meet me on the beach in fifteen minutes." M left the beach house, casing their surroundings.

Madison had finally succumbed, handing her control to the tides. She would need a deeper strength. She knew M had returned to her life, the beach for much more than a visit.

The waves pounded against the shore, a subtle litany. Soft sea bubbles massaged Madison's ankles and toes. The day sang through nature as the sun began to climb and shine, warming the shivers Madison couldn't seem to shake. M was walking toward Madison swinging her arms with that genetic sway Madison had long missed. As the two women approached each other, there seemed a cacophony of energies swirling between their bosoms. The two embraced as those electric shivers rushed Madison's spine. The scent of her mother's lavender laundry detergent blew in the gentle breeze between them.

"Was that…?" Madison looked at M with eloquent disbelief.

"It's hello." Her mother had raced through M's touch. In their embrace, M felt slight pangs of change, sensed differences in Madison's receptivity to her ways.

"When are you going to tell me why you are really here, M?" Madison spoke in generalities, afraid that the seagulls might be spies. The walls and sea creatures listened when they were together.

"When you are finally ready to listen to more than just me." M's eyes were firm, motherly.

"What does that even mean?!" Madison tried to play the outsider, but that slipper wasn't fitting. M saw right through her charade.

"You know what I mean. You have always fought things that try to teach you." M watched Madison's lip turn downward, that stubborn, helpless child she knew long ago.

"This person following us tonight... Is it tied to me?" M and Madison walked, watching the purple mix with the golden sunlight. Their breaths laced with skulls and crossbones as their bodies casually swayed.

"We are all tied to you, Madison." M's eyes went off someplace far and terrifyingly familiar to Madison.

The beach was their only safe place to know things.

Gabriella Lowe Vandeven

I'm not your typical twenty-year-old. I'm not a slave to the rhythm of technology. You won't see me burning up my phone with social media and snap chat, tweets, or Facebook like all the other poor zombies who never knew something more. I'm an old soul. I grew up around adults who didn't find technology quite so romantic. Don't get me wrong, my father is a technology genius, but he isn't addicted to it. My father bought the house for me. He hoped it could give me some firm foundations. He is a security expert. He's all about surety. He protects the very well-known not with his stature, but with his brilliant use of technology. My mother, Gabrielle, is a researcher. She has had Multiple Sclerosis her whole adult life, so her occupation is fitting. It takes her all over the world. My parents have never truly lived together. They live out of a suitcase as I did most of my childhood. I bounced from parent to parent, place to place. This beach house is my anchored home. It was my mother's childhood vacation home that her parents left to some neighborhood kids they loved.

I've always known things. Things I don't know why or how I knew. My mother has the same knowing. She'd utter the words I was thinking. It was a symbiosis I have always found eternal. As a child, I frequently asked her about the gray people that lived with us. My mother never did anything but encourage me to embrace that ability because one day it would matter to me. We all have that ability to communicate with God, angels, and those who have moved on. It is unique to us all, but especially for those touched most by death.

I am a massage therapist and I help people with more than their physicality. My mother taught me to use my power for good. I sense that she had a lot of darkness in her own past. Lots of death. She said some things are better left buried as long as the lessons are learned, the patterns never repeated. I have to learn my life lessons my way.

I've grown very close with Madison and her entourage next door. There's a lot of death in their postures. Lots of powerful gray that protects them. I found Houston on the beach as he lay dying, his soul rushed through me as he exited his physicality. He was a firm, kind man who had a lot of influence. I never understood his relationship with Madison. I sense she has some mighty skeletons hidden. Madison and Dyer are very kind and inclusive of me. They take care of outsiders. They've been the outsiders. Aunt M, as Hannah calls her, is much more. She was a detective, so that explains her poker-faced wisdom. She is someone to know and trust and I like having her around when she visits Madison. Hannah is an old soul looking for that childhood that was stolen. She talks to me about the flashes she still gets of very evil things. We both need a place to be that child we lost. My mom's old childhood room is our perfect safe place.

My parents were always estranged and strange. I didn't understand it until I saw my mother disappear before my very eyes. She time travels. That's my Norman Rockwell life.

Wallflowers

Walls so empty
Made anew
Never denying
What is true.

Walls so humble
Strength respite
Built to house
Another plight.

Walls so blank
They just cry.
Only the walls
Can say why.

Walls so steadfast
Superb
Singing stories
Selling verbs.

Walls a sanctuary
Or a doom.
Only the sage
Knows the room.

Dreamweaver

Humility doesn't come sized and boxed in specifics. It creeps into the essence of our bits of goodness, the parts of ourselves we listen to on the good days. It transcends pride and humanity with personal honesty. In the night when most are afraid of the dark, our unconscious takes the opportunity to take us out of our own darkness. It redirects our waking stresses with positive, guided scenarios that our soul understands and will be most receptive to hearing. Our egos have to tell stories that pad and cushion our truths. The ones we can't see in our waking hours with much clarity.

The dreams started for Madison after her mother died. She never dreamed of her mother until her death. As a child, Madison had always had vivid memories of her nightly brushes with the waves and wind. These new dreams were more than a memory. They were a portal to a place just above humanity where the living and the dead tether close and commune. Madison found her mother that honest mirror she could look into that truly gauged the uncomfortable in her own life and mind.

Madison was stubborn and wouldn't always accept the gift of insight. Some nights the dreams turned fierce or chilling, anything to get her to look and listen. Madison had skills. She just tried to control the gifts or put them in her pocket for the storms of living. She hadn't realized that life was a storm you navigated rather than fought.

The chaos of Houston's sudden death washed out with the tides, leaving subtle voids in Madison and the children's normal day. They were strangers in their own family. They would all make it through the day to find misplaced emptiness and confusion as the sun set. Everyone seemed to scatter after the mechanics of the day were done as if the others' grief was a burden rather than a common thread.

Madison had returned to counseling at the hospital. She had only taken on a few cases of children who had lost their parents, knowing their grief would reopen her own, but in healing ways. Madison spent many an evening on the porch with Dyer and Peck. Peck, a joyful reminder of his father, unaware in those first few months what death truly entailed. He had Dyer and Madison and his folly and innocence floated their sadness. Hannah had been the most withdrawn, seeking friendship with the neighbor, Lowe. Lowe was in her early twenties, just the sort of energy Hannah wanted to be around as a blossoming teenager. Hannah was having a hard time coping with her guilt. She had wished Houston gone from their lives and magically her wish was granted in the most horrible of fashions. She felt like God was teaching her an awfully hard lesson in love.

Some days were fluid and tiny glints of hope appeared in random smiles. Today had been heavy, leaving Madison guarded and aloof. The water rained rhythmically from the shower head down onto Madison's neck, carving sinewy paths down her spine and leg, fluid like rapid currents that follow a river creek bed. Dyer heard her sighing, hiding in the blankness of the water. He put his open palm on the shower door and her crooked fingers joined his, separated only by glass. They had spent the afternoon alone, skin to skin, silencing the world and the circumstances. It was imperative that they have one day a week that nothing mattered but intimacy. These days were healthy and honest. Madison was able to release a lot of fear and self-loathing. Some weeks it was harder to find. Madison was good at putting up walls with tricky locks.

Dyer's sincerity brought out the beauty she held tightly inside. He understood her need to protect her very sensitive skin. Madison slid into the bed beside Dyer, her hair damp, her neck fragrant with signature pheromones. They had shared bits of true pleasure, lying still, saying nothing, sensing everything.

The rolling cemetery looked familiar. A lone tree that was easily one hundred years old had commanded the headstones to stand at attention. Madison was standing at the top of this old cemetery she hadn't visited in eons. It was spring because the grass was lime green and new. In Madison's left ear she hears *It won't be long*. It startled her. She knew the voice and it hit a chord that triggered nostalgic timelessness. Madison turned her head to the words and Houston stood to her left, his shoulder touching hers as he surveyed the view.

"What are you doing here?" Madison was aware Houston was dead.

"Yes, I'm dead. But what you don't know is how…that I was murdered." Houston glanced at Madison with a loaded grin so reminiscent.

"I don't understand." Madison tried to play coy with the knowledge. Houston now appeared to her right, forcing her vision to a freshly buried grave.

"Madison, dear, I think you do." They seemed to talk without moving their lips.

The dream changed scenes. Madison was in their suite at the Capital Hotel, looking out the window at rain moving in sheets to the ground that seemed far, far below. This place represented a time Houston had chosen to help Madison many years ago. A time when none of them were perfect or even good people at this juncture. This hotel was where their shared aversion and attempted escape from mafia ties had played out poorly. She could hear Houston shaving in the bathroom, his razor hummed like an incessant fly. He emerged from the bathroom, razor still buzzing until it found Madison. The razor stopped abruptly as the dream scene became a series of summarized blurbs from that fateful day they all went very dark to find the light. People died, police turned deaf ears, money disappeared. But not the shadowy cohort.

It had been elusive and patient and would never relent.

"It's always going to be dangerous, Madison." Madison heard Houston's words float in over her shoulder with an odd clarity.

"Will it end?" Madison felt cold and hopeless.

"When you lose." She turned to face Houston and he was blurry and more distant than his voice. Conversations in dreams like these were between souls. His face changed ages as the dream advanced, his features soft and fuzzy.

Madison's limbs twitched in violent unison as she abruptly awoke. The threat was always going to be out there, eating at her sense of well-being. Madison focused on Houston's words...*murdered...I think you do... When you lose*...M was here because Houston was murdered. She opened her eyes and felt gravity, heaviness that was weighted once again with her fears. Yet, the familiarity that now enveloped her was comforting, as if she had just visited with Houston. His presence was all around her and there was a peaceable energy he fondly conjured that tickled her stomach. She looked to Dyer sleeping beside her and she knew Houston was watching over all of them. Madison knew she had to find the end.

Dallas

Funerals for family were draining. Funerals for family in other family's city under other people's skies was daunting. Houston's daughter had made the graveside simple, honorable. Still, she could hear her father shout expletives. It was the Dallas attendees that mucked up the honor part. The haughty elite that Houston had known back in the1980's oil days made their presence with diamonds, big hair, Botox - old money. Madison and Houston's other life with all the common people made Madison the fish out of water in this setting. Madison missed the tides. She cared little for the pomp and circumstance of southern societal floggings.

The service was Texas-style, likened to pistols at thirty paces with Houston's casket the proverbial line in the dirt. Madison had a small flock of her own representing Houston's second act. Madison's front line of defense was Dyer who steadied Peck's shoulders. Hannah stood between Madison and M. Tiered behind them were Lowe and her mother Gabrielle. The other friends peppered the small triangle they had formed. On the other side of the casket stood the haughty elite. M held Madison's hand, concerting their loving energy, providing a white light of hope. M saw the negative, self-loathing shadows that hovered over many of the plastic privileged. Elitists emanated fear. M made sure it had little effect on Madison's motley crew of beautiful hues bonded by their differences.

The final song was sung, the roses were placed just so, and the coffin was lowered. The

Dallas brood flipped the switch; their tear ducts suddenly dry. They turned to each other with arrogant chatter, smug and superficial, ignoring Madison's side of the coffin. It was a melody of ire. One more bitter pill for Madison to swallow. The Hispanic burial attendant, who didn't speak English, but certainly sarcasm, grinned at Madison's crew as he shoveled very plain dirt into a very expensive hole.

M Factor

M had always been in the death business. She moved through the little deaths in her life that no one saw or understood into the larger, more serious milestones in a life well lived. She moved from police officer to detective and in the years following her sister's death, she worked the cold cases. Cases where death never had a period at the end and suffering and circumstances played in a loop. She had many loops of her own that fueled her need to help others. She had gotten good at deciphering cues surrounding death. M was keen to the suffering of others, could pull it out of human behaviors or ill-structured stories. She had a nose like a canine for truth. M had a great degree of anonymity about her, an empathy people were comfortable around. It made her ear well-worn and she used those skills to sheer off the facade vs the genuine. No one knew the depths inside her mind and the many times she solved issues or cases by giving the right information the right people. This let the right people make the right deductions. She did not enjoy recognition. She enjoyed teaching others how to recognize. Being brushed by death very personally, M appreciated the gifts her life had to offer to others. She hadn't always felt as if her near death experience was an opportunity. It had rattled her sense of self. It forced her to go deeper and acknowledge the talents she could use as a tool.

Madison had the same sort of skill set, yet M watched Madison fail miserably at giving these whispers sincere credence. Madison had been more firmly grounded most of her life and it took her mistake after tragedy to finally accept the life that was being handed to her. M had stood back and waited for the right time to reenter Madison's journey. She couldn't push her way into people's hearts. It was by circumstances surrounding death that M had mastered walking into someone's very personal life. Lives that had been upended by something horrific and then getting those wounded people to trust her with their vulnerability. M was loyal.

The walls had ears. M hadn't been able to verbalize to Madison all the reasons she was here, now. These truths regarding Madison's past had been fragmented and unclear to M through the years. Some facts just hadn't added up - until Houston's death.

M looked at the photos of all those murdered. Houston and Dyer's first wife had been poisoned. Killed to make it look conveniently natural. A well-timed, well-plotted departure by a puppeteer. All killed by association to Madison Peacock. M felt warm tears of frustration forming in her eyes.

M opened the file and stared at his picture. She knew death confidentially and had always sensed that his face hadn't died the sort of death he deserved. No, he never really died. He concocted a cowardly death that was motivated by greed and narcissism. These deaths were about controlling Madison. Her stomach roiled with dingy fear. Forever, that eminent danger in All their lives. They were merely strings attached wearing manipulative nooses of guilt he had artfully placed around all of their necks. Felt even in their stillness. Madison would soon learn the truths around all this death, why M was reconnecting now.

January – May
2015

Giving In

M stayed close to Madison, protecting her perimeter. She watched her niece tidy up phases of her life into neat packages. In the months following the funeral, Madison had resorted to old ways of coping. She put everyone in boxes and at arms-length. Madison was so sensitive the slightest touches signaled tsunami waves of old verbiage that took over her rationale.

M was staying with Lowe a few doors down. These two strange women, very different ages with mad proclivities, had hit it off after Houston's funeral. Lowe was becoming a bright shining star in M's days on the beach. The kinship between them was nourishing. M looked forward to knowing Lowe better, to knowing them all. M doted on taking care of both households, finding home the hearts that dwelled inside.

Hannah finished off her afternoons visiting with M about her dramatic days as a teenager in junior high. Peck bounded bombastically, enjoying

M's undivided doting. M yearned, had missed this. She knew this quelled a familiar emptiness all of them felt in their shattered families. It was filling the terrible with the simple, kind, and mundane. Both families sat down to dinner a few evenings a week. More meals and banter, establishing a new normal to muffle the strange silences.

Nothing could quell the awkward pauses today. Dyer had taken the kids for the Saturday. Lowe and M had gone for coffee. Everyone had tasted Madison's soured mood and had left her alone. Madison was a powder keg. She had just finished boxing up the last of Houston's things, suddenly aware the boxes were in the same corner as his suitcases. The official space where Houston exits in every respect.

Lowe and M spoke in hushed verbs as they walked into the beach house. Madison's gaze gravitated to their voices, her eyes lost in a place she did not share.

"It's a beautiful day. You should walk the beach." Lowe and M poked at her personal space with idle chit chat, hoping not to ignite her.

"I should do a lot of things." Madison's shoulders were under her earlobes, her mind toxic. She was holding back, pushing back as her body pushed forward.

"You look like hell, Madison." M threw the match only igniting bad memories Madison and M shared. Death was that rickety turning point in their paths that they talked little about.

"Why don't you let me do some therapy on you." Lowe was a peacemaker.

"What are you two up to?" Madison knew her aunt knew things she hid in the whites of her eyes.

Madison had memorized how M interacted with Gabrielle and her daughter, Lowe, after the funeral in Dallas. M had walked along side Madison's mother and her with a similar, subtle ease.

"GO with Lowe." M grabbed Madison's plastic grip and joined her palm with Lowe's. Human touch instantly soothed, dissolved defenses.

"You need to be ready for surprises." Lowe chuckled as she squeezed Madison's hand.

"I don't do surprises." Madison's acerbic smirk contorted as her body screamed for feeling.

"Give in, Madison. Your body will do the rest." M always cradled others well, making them feel comfortable.

"That is what I am afraid of…" Madison frowned as Lowe coaxed her to the door.

The rigidity fell away a bit. Madison let other hands carry her weariness.

"Thanks for trusting me, Madison." M grinned as Madison rounded the corner. M's crooked lips always spoke truths.

Truisms

Madison's body was disciplined. Lowe had to fight its tight, concise machinations. The first therapy session would be about trust. Touch the ultimate trust, for Madison was a woman who controlled the only things she had ever been able to in her life, her reactions. When Lowe had finally put Madison in a safe mode, her body fell into its natural rhythm that was fluid and robust, working with and not against Lowe's touch.

Madison exhaled her woe in trance language that few related. It was raw and expressive, all that she couldn't be in her waking hours. Lowe knew Madison was upon a precipice she would have to lean and fumble towards. Her body now had the instructions, the road map. It was now Madison's job to befriend all the Pandora's boxes she had compartmentalized her life into with wicked precision. It would be a messy unearthing of lost voices she had stymied in order to survive. It was now essential that she listen in order to live any sort of authentic life.

Madison unlocked the front door and the echo of the key in the lock sent flashes of memory through M's mind. It was an instantaneous blurb, just out of her reach like many of her dreams. M heard Madison's footsteps. They touted less gravity. The two locked stares, studying the other. Genetic language passed.

"You've been having those dreams again, haven't you?" M sniffed her sister all around Madison.

"Yes." Madison sank beside her aunt. Her stature humbled. She noticed M's half empty glass of liquor. It smelled of wonderful dark rum in the jet stream between their breaths.

"She's everywhere, M." Madison felt phantom tears again, but this time she couldn't stop them. M offered her the rest of her cocktail as she smiled nostalgically.

"Good. Really listen to her this time." M could feel the bands around Madison's control a bit looser and more receptive.

Madison looked around the condo that was now beginning to take on a shape and form she had never really broached; it was looking like a portrait of her life rather than a palette of others. For a moment she felt proud, almost confident again.

"What is this surprise?" Madison's gaze twinkled with hints of her mother's curiosity. She noticed there were no kids, no noise.

"This." M perched her ear to the silence. "Lowe and I will have the kids next door for the night. This quiet is yours tonight…do whatever you want."

"I don't know what to say…" Madison's boxed anger over her mother's death had made her abandon her aunt once, long ago. M's kind gesture fed the regret Madison oozed.

"Say you'll get out of your own way a bit. Let the kids just be. You just let life come to you."

M had Madison by the heartstrings for the first time since she was a little girl.

"Why do you care so?" Madison watched her aunt's eyes soften as her truisms flowed.

"Someone's got to love you, honey. You are doing a lousy job of it yourself right now. Quit pushing everyone away." The ice in M's glass shifted swiftly with a ping of affirmation from spirit fingers nearby.

"I've always needed you." Madison reached for M, feeling her heart beat in sloshy sync with her own.

"I've always been close, dear." M kissed Madison on the side of her mouth. It was a maternal gesture M had always showered upon Madison. It always made Madison feel special.

Madison was visibly lighter in spirit. M could tell Madison was trying to let her self-imposed shackles fall slack. The air in the condo was breathable again. Old things still haunted both of their depths, but not in frightening fashions.

The lingering threats they harbored were equated to old friends just passing through – at least for now.

Madison poured a glass of sweet, dark rum and started a very hot bath. M tidied up the remaining packing scraps scattered about the living room. She noticed the boxes of Houston's belongings packed up, stacked, and numbered 1,2,3,4,5,6 – a perfect order of steps, unconsciously encouraging Madison.

As the bathroom faucet shut off to silence, M scribbled a note that read *Call Dyer*. She sensed Madison was one step ahead of her. Dyer was good for her niece.

M closed the front door and engaged the dead bolt, a flicker of an audible sound raced her balance. This time she recognized the audible vocal. She smiled as goose bumps rose up her spine. She blew air kisses in the direction of her sister's energy that had lauded her.

Hitting the Wall

Dyer found Madison asleep in the bathtub. The water was lukewarm, but effective, her mouth agape. He listened to her snore, naked as a happy newborn, wrapped in a water blanket.

Maybe she was flat exhausted after making love to a brawny, tall, dark rum drink? Dyer surmised jealously, sniffing her empty glass. It had definitely warmed her toes with lover's contentment.

Dyer was so frustrated. Maybe he should have left her alone, but her odd stoniness the past few months had him confused. Was he just her reflex, an old habit? He and Madison had crossed into a healthy place together, had made some plans for the future when all this death collapsed on her again. The Madison he had known fought, she moved, she didn't retreat. Dyer had seen her at her finest and her worst in their brief lifetime of drama. Somehow, he wanted to tap into the other parts of her, all the rest.

Her sweaty, melted glass sat on the edge of the tub, awaiting Dyer's invitation. With his frustration, he poured the melted rum on the base of Madison's throat. The melt rushed down between her cleavage, past her heart, splintering at her belly button. Nothing. She snorted only slightly.

Dyer wanted to throttle the changes out of her. He relented to stare tactics, propping his chin on the side of the tub and boring his presence into her forehead with his brown sugar eyes. Olfactory wiggled her nose. It smelled his skin in her space.

Madison's eyes fluttered open with a crocodile connection to his stare. It was almost a telepathic moment that grew grins from them both. They didn't move anything but their eyes that rivaled the other very sensually.

"Surprise." Dyer leaned dangerously over the tub, into her cheekbone, kissing her temple, her nose.

Dyer ran a finger through her wet, matted hair, twirling it in circular motions. Madison sobbed as he kissed the corner of her wide smile. Dyer was tearing away the walls she constructed, one brick at a time.

Like the flick of a switch, Madison pulled Dyer into the bathtub with her. Dyer stood like a wet giant, boots and jeans, in the bath. His eyes saucers of disbelief. Madison's tears turned to cackles. Dyer pulled Madison from the bath and into his arms and his vulnerability. They laughed, they kissed. Dyer hoped she'd one day see herself as he did. Until that day, he'd move love through her rather than take it away.

"Come on, Madison." Dyer could feel Madison's heart charging her blood through her weary frame. Her soul was very tactile, working through the layers of reason she had gauzed herself in.

"What's going on in your head?" Dyer had been her whipping boy many years ago and he knew how she worked. He had to coax her out of herself.

"I want to hit things – hard!" Madison crumbled his shirt into her fists as she gritted her teeth.

"Do it." Dyer egged her rage. He could feel her kneading his shirt in her fists, about to pop.

Madison slapped Dyer across the face. Dyer could see the explosion ignite. A tirade of pent fury for those men who had wronged her, left her a lame animal once. He felt her rage.

"I'm sorry." Madison regretted her reaction, pulling back.

"Sorry for what?" Dyer strong-armed her, made her own her thorns. Dyer pressed her in that buffered space between them.

"For putting you through me. I'm afraid of myself." Madison winced. "I don't know this angry, sad woman."

"This woman is just grieving. She's you. She's beautiful. You just have to let her happen." Dyer watched Madison bend toward his words.

Madison now fidgeted with the buttons on his shirt. She contemplated the consequences of this sort of permission. This time, this man, there were none.

"I don't know how. I don't deserve you." Madison began unbuttoning Dyer's shirt in slow stops and starts, training wheels. He kissed her nakedness with loving affirmation.

"Wrong." Dyer stomped his boots off and lifted her out of the long cold bath water.

Dyer had always watched Madison, with fine precision, honed her self-restraint and birth a blob of all that plagued her. She molded the ilk into something firth she and all she loved could rely upon. This time Dyer wanted to be the one Madison could rely upon.

"This strange woman, she needs you, you know?" Madison slid her fingers into Dyer's back jean pockets, pulling him closer to her. Consent was humbling. She had never felt braver in her life for being true to her feelings.

"Good. Cause she's going to get me." Dyer started shedding his clothes as they fumbled to the floor. They kissed like hungry teenagers, driven by their hormones. This that develpoed was much more than lust.

There was an invisible line that they had never crossed, a place they reserved privately in their eye contact. A lovely trust was forming. A trust easily breeched in the past by both their others who didn't respect boundaries. Dyer and Madison's toes finally dared this margin.

Syncopation strengthened that quiet force between them. Time would prove that their longing fed their bond. Nothing had ever conquered it. It fused their souls in dear ways they didn't question. Death would not be their traitor. Meant-to-be endured the trials of loss and disappointment.

Carpet Pizza

Madison and Dyer passed lovers' banter in their words and actions, taking space for what they had created and giving it breath and life. They spent the better half of the evening talking, existing in same air, watching the flicker of white noise from the television. They moved their mood to the living room and cooked "carpet" pizza. Peck had coined the phrase "carpet pizza" for this tradition. When Peck was a toddler, every time they'd cooked pizza, they'd all sit on the floor together at Peck's level and eat. From then on, Peck started asking for "carpet pizza." It had become cherished and stuck with them all.

Private time together was always imperfect. Life and death had made it more sporadic. Especially this death. Madison had made excuses born of her own fears of the sides of herself she hid. She didn't trust what came out of her own mouth. The waves had been particularly vocal with sunset. They had cracked a window to listen to the tide's conversations. Even the January breezes were laced with humidity that swirled a thickness, enveloping them with unspoken. She couldn't convince herself that Dyer would totally accept these new parts she juggled and doled when opportune. All the men in her life had put her misnomers in a black frame and expected her to be Mona Lisa. When she wasn't congruent with their ideals, she was tossed into a big box and labeled "bitch" because they didn't know how to handle her.

Dyer was sitting on the floor with his arms crossed, his back propped against the couch. Madison's heavy thoughts rested on his blue jeaned lap. The only sounds heard were clocks that ticked, wind that whistled through the open window, and the waves that crashed and startled with cymbal precision.

Madison opened her blue eyes and looked upward at him. He looked like a giant, his long torso appearing miles high. His lips pursed and his head bobbed as he fought sleep. They were pleasantly drained of energy. Yet, their selfishness seemed to move Madison's guilt up and down her conscience.

"Dyer, the kids - they are messier than us if that is possible." Madison could feel Peck's frenetic energy through the walls two houses down. It was almost as volatile as Hannah's raging preteen moods. They were all riding the titanic of grief.

"Please feel something other than guilt. Just let the kids feel. They've got to learn that life isn't fair. You are a good mother." Dyer spoke his peace, his lips funny looking upside down from Madison's view. Madison admired his robust, yet tender chosen words.

"Am I a good mother? I wonder. I was pretty rotten to my own mother before she died. I've been dreaming of her again." Madison dropped a little snippet of her inner life to him.

"If I were a betting man, I'd say your mother must have been persistent and independent?" Dyer fished for validation.

"Marcella was a stubborn detective. But she would have liked you." Madison's eyes softened as her mother's name rolled off her lips. It seemed to have disappeared with her death, becoming an expletive in their family.

"Duh." Dyer smirked.

"She comes to me in dreams, guides me... like she is working a case. I don't know what she's trying to tell me. It's like there is more of this death coming." Madison knew most rational men were closed off to the places she was treading.

"You, me, and dead people. You can't be afraid. The math always adds up." Dyer breathed in her admonitions.

"Yeah, do this math and see if it adds up." Madison was an anomaly that life used to teach all who listened.

"Math is math. I don't need dead people to tell me that." Dyer connected her dots nicely, loving the anxiety they exhaled in their laughter.

Dyer rolled her head of mopped hair off his thighs. He flipped on top of her, pinning her wrists above her head. He challenged her will as she tried to Houdini away from his candor. Dyer kissed the nape of her neck.

"I trust you and your dead things, Madison." Dyer grunted in cave man fashion. He separated her knees and lowered his body close to hers.

"Good. Cause I don't." Madison giggled and grunted her own primal signal, wrestling her intuition, that had a foot in the now and the spirit places she bobbled.

"Thank you, thank you." Madison whispered repeatedly, a mantra filling their long, pregnant silence.

"No, thank you for letting us have some time between your legs." Dyer pinched her pointed nose closed and she screamed with a beautiful agony that he loved.

"I did participate." There were little cuts in Madison's voice.

"Yes...so were a lot of other things." Dyer looked deep past her eyes at her reaction to his honesty.

"Ah, and you're still here. Either you're pretty amazing or just desperate." Madison chortled defensively.

"Desperate for all of you, and your odd things." Dyer loosened his grip on her wrists, half expecting her to slap him again.

"Let's get out of my head." Madison trembled, her chest rising high as she sighed a long unsteady exhale.

Dyer rubbed his stubbly cheek to hers. Madison wrapped her long legs around his waist, beckoning closeness, threading the two of them together. Her open mouth searched for his kisses. He loved watching her learn trust.

Those Dreams

Dyer and Madison spoke a language that couldn't be totally translated. Madison had shared her raging guilt over Houston's death through a series of sexual combats. Dyer hadn't minded that she took out her frustration in fitful bouts of lust. Once inelegantly sufficed, Madison crashed with the brevity of a led zeppelin, taking Dyer and her control down with her, splintered in emoted debris.

He watched Madison's face mourn those men before him and for different reasons each time. Dyer had flogged Madison with his own misplaced anger more than once in regard to his own abysmal losses. Madison had known how to harness and channel his intentions, pacified his angst.

Dyer recognized her body's commanding drum beat rhythm that tamed and soothed her agony. Yet, he couldn't pacify her grief. Madison had learned how to harden her tender skin so that even Dyer's softest caresses couldn't infiltrate her.

Dyer pulled at the distance of her taut body. A body that fought to allow itself to feel more than only the anger. She was so wrapped into the thick cocoon she had spun that she could no longer find even a thin seam to escape.

Dyer wasn't prepared, though, for those dreams of hers. Madison slept particularly hard and loud. She talked in her sleep like a sniveling child. She called out to her mother more than once. She kicked and punched at the bullies, those that had changed her landscape. She wasn't ready to accept their legacies without some concessions. Dyer wondered what those dreams she had eluded to were now doling upon her.

"NO!" Madison raised straight up in their bed, fisting the darkness. Dyer tackled her back to her pillow.

"I hate you for leaving me… Don't ambush me… pity…I loved you…Why…?" Madison whimpered and began speaking in inaudible, mumbled fragments.

"Madison, wake up." Dyer cupped her cheek in one beefy palm as he roused her with the other.

Madison opened an unresponsive eye, instinctively grounding her whereabouts.

"What were you dreaming?" Dyer's palms were now firmly holding her cheeks. Her tears met his brawny palms.

"People always leave." Madison rolled away from Dyer. He spooned her sobs, wrapping his compassion firmly around her.

"Why not let them go?" Dyer squeezed her close to his beating heart. Madison turned to face his words.

"Because I'm afraid…." The unbroken and honest in her began to flow. "and I'm raw…I can't do it again."

"Of what?" Something was rattling her. Madison was never this cold and full of self-deprecation.

"I can't lose anymore right now." Dyer understood their tension better.

"Then just love." Dyer wiped her tears, kissing her snotty nose.

"I love you, Dyer. I've always been in love with you." Madison closed her eyes and tears zigzagged down her fine lines.

"I love you for all the right reasons, Ms. Peacock." It finally escaped his lips.

Dyer had wanted to tell Madison how much he loved her that first night they were officially to be a couple. The infamous night Houston died rather than leaving the scene. Dyer respected Madison by being her safety, not her savior.

Dyer and Madison slept close, their elbows and feet touching each other at all times. The lifeline that connected their blood flow. Dyer had dug out the woman he believed in for so long. He wasn't going to let her forget that soul he understood in strange ways.

Gaggle of Gals – May 2015

The decibel peak of all possible exists when there are at least two females huddled together, their eyes stars and diamonds. They seem to solve all the problems of their worlds by simply expressing them. They dream vividly, their words a needle and thread working a fabric of their making with beautiful ideals. Ideals that will ultimately sustain them when they are shattered with life's disillusions.

Each of our lives holds the bigger picture we cannot see when we are young and malleable. Malleable lets us soak up those home senses. Our truest selves we will inherently know forever. The young learn equal, internalize that which is said versus what is done. Only when all the adults start falling off their pedestals and dropping their crowns will the naïve graduate into true humanity. That or deny their truths and perpetuate the lovely chains of hypocrisy. Thankfully, life has lips that sweetly encourage the young and old to move toward the higher roads, beyond their egos. Life is as receptively nonjudgmental as it is beautifully flawed.

The board game LIFE, grandiose, fashioned in the 1980's when excess reigned, centered the retro room. It's cards and game pieces abandoned abruptly for other endeavors. It gave this ancient, unused space charm and breath once again. The room had a mystical charm that drew people to it. It was a forever space. Hannah sat in the window, reading an old book she found on the desk, *Catcher in the Rye*. The inside cover had written in rainbow ink: Property of G.V. It struck rebellious chords she could play. She had been reading it every afternoon she came by to see Lowe. Today, Hannah finished the book, relating to the last sentence…*Don't tell anybody anything. If you do, you start missing everybody.*

Lowe was finishing her massage therapy for the day. The man had MS like her mother, Gabby. Lowe had always taken special care of her MS patients in the ways she never could her own mother. She had noticed how difficult his left side had been at responding. It was spastic and almost schizophrenic in its nerve firing. He had just suddenly lost his wife of 30 years. His grief had played out through his strangely wrecked nervous system, sending him at times to sobbing tears he couldn't parlay. His wife had been his caregiver, had encouraged him to seek this sort of therapy for his pains. This man's wife was a lovely shade of purple that hovered beside him the whole therapy session. Lowe imbibed the beautiful rhythm she infused into her ailing husband. It left Lowe feeling magnificently refreshed herself.

Lowe knocked three times on the loft bedroom door that had once been her mother's secret escape as a teen. It was now their code, their new tradition since late October. Hannah opened the door to find Lowe with two bottles of Coca Cola in hand. They sat on the floor beside the abandoned board game and drank the cokes as the afternoon sunlight spotlighted particular portions of fading colors in the well worn room. Lowe noticed the book in Hannah's hand.

"Did you finish?" Lowe watched Hannah turn her coke skyward.

"I did." Hannah belched and they covered their mouths, laughing like kids, hoping the coke wouldn't come out their noses.

"Well, what did you think of it?" Lowe had loved that book.

"I think Holden and I would be good friends. I get him, totally." Hannah's blue eyes fell back into the pages of Holden's rambling storytelling.

"You keep the book. It's my mother's favorite as well." Lowe looked around the room and Gabby, the rebel, spoke in this odd loft space frozen in the 70's and 80's.

"You don't think she'd mind?" Hannah felt like Lowe's mom was just one of the girls, cool and ageless, not a mother with rules.

"She'd insist." Lowe drank her coke, watching Hannah's face out of the corner of her eye. Something was off.

"So what's up?" Lowe noticed the dark shadow of a fatherly man that often hovered directly behind Hannah's aura. He kept a long, familial distance.

"I'm seeing that creepy man again in my dreams. It's like a memory. Can you see him?" This was their thing. Hannah and Lowe shared more than Coca Cola.

"No creepy man. I see a different man. It feels fatherly, like he could be a guardian angel. Maybe Houston?" Hannah looked around the room, wishing she understood the things that were happening to her. Things that seemed to happen when people around her died.

"Don't tell my mother! She doesn't get this kind of thing. She'd try to analyze me to death." Hannah anxiously sifted through the cards that went to the game.

"Don't be so sure. People are more off than on. That stuff is normal to me." Lowe was so glad that Hannah shared with her. Hannah would learn that everyone is touched by the "in between" at some death point in their lives.

"Your mom is a super cool gypsy." Hannah flicked a card at Lowe. Lowe flicked one back at Hannah.

It slipped between the old board flooring. They both noticed it stopped halfway. They had lost thousands of small toys and trinkets to the gaps in the past that seemed to fall into an abyss.

"What is up with that?" Hannah's mind went other worldly. Lowe grabbed a flashlight. She shone the light between the boards and noticed the card had stuck on something metal.

"There's something down there." They lean in closely, focusing on the board. There's a knock on the door and the girls bump heads, screeching like cats.

"Pray tell? Or do I want to know?" They turned around to find M standing in the doorway.

M grinned with intention that startled Lowe. Lowe noticed that brilliant twin shadow that always stayed fused with M. It seemed to delight in their fright.

Something about Hannah's aunt had always been – endearing – that was the word that came to Lowe.

Something Metal

The quest had begun to uncover that something metal under the floorboards. When M retired for the evening, Hannah and Lowe returned to the loft. They twisted and contorted with the flashlight, poked at the mystery with a pencil, but got nothing more than a metallic sound.

"Maybe we could pry the board up?" Hannah was looking around the room as if a crowbar was part of the decorum.

"This is here on purpose. There has to be a way in." Lowe studied the board, pressing and prying it in various corners as if it had a James Bond release mechanism.

"Let's ask Siri." Hannah pulled her phone from her pocket and noticed she had two missed calls from her mother and a text that read: Be home by 9pm. It was already 8:30 pm.

"Cat got Siri's tongue?" Lowe noticed Hannah texting, her fingers racing curfew.

"My mother. She wants me home just when things are getting good!" Hannah stomps the floor as she sends her text reply.

The whole board of the floor flew up, a perfectly cut portion, undetectable. It rose with precision, hinged and all. Under the board was a long, deep black metal box that looked fireproof or could be used as a tool box. Shielded by the upended board, Lowe grabbed a note off the top of box without detection and slid it into her pocket.

She slammed down the board as quickly as it flew up, as if it were criminal. It clicked masterfully.

"Lowe, what just happened?" Hannah froze, afraid the place was a walking boobie trap.

"We'll have to investigate things tomorrow. You'd better go home." Hannah's phone chimed several text replies from her mother. Lowe gave Hannah a nod. Hannah ran down the stairs and out the door. Lowe locked the loft door, intrigued. She retrieved the folded letter from her shirt pocket.

A Letter to My Daughter

My Lowe,

I knew one day you'd find this box in divine right timing. It's how it works for us. We communicate rather uniquely. Just know that once you delve into the box, there is no turning back. But, I think since you are reading this letter now, you are ready.

I didn't know what to think of your red hair when you were born. I have very dark hair and so does your father, so red made me question the nurse if she had handed me someone else's child. You yawned and I saw my dimples sink in your cheeks and for the first time in my whole life, someone looked like me, someone was mine. You may have suspected it or maybe I taught you better. Family is what you create more than genetics.

I was adopted at birth. My mother wanted children badly and couldn't have them, but she and my father couldn't conceive. She worked at a hospital and saw lots of unwed pregnant teen girls come through that put their children up for adoption. When I was born, she helped deliver me. She said the young woman didn't know what to do, had hidden her pregnancy from her family. She was only fifteen. Mother adopted me and I knew nothing about being adopted until I was a teenager. My father was psychotic, a brilliant doctor who had a god complex and he was abusive to me when I found out I had MS. He did all kinds of experiments on me trying to "cure" me. The life my birth mother tried to give me turned out to be a tragic one that always left me wondering "why me?" What good am I supposed to do with this life I've been challenged by?

I made a lot of bad choices in my youth. I ran with some criminals I thought were innovators. I escaped my father but never escaped that prisoner mindset. Your father and I were romantically a flash in the pan – and then there was you. We did not live a typical married life. You have always tethered us. You were the first face I could look at and see myself, my mannerisms, my spirit. You healed a lot of the wounds I kept ripping open with self-doubt. I promised I'd raise you like my birth mother couldn't. I'd love you and always make you feel accepted. I'd give you diversity and culture, humility and compassion. I'd try to mold the Lowe that would go and make her own mistakes and way. 'Cause you will falter and you will fail. But, I will always

unconditionally love you and be that force around
you – living or dead. You are mine, are made from
me, so we will forever be.

It was only after my own mother died that I
began to search for my birth mother. I wanted a
face to go with all the scenarios I had imagined
growing up. I needed to know her. I had
questions only she could pacify. Every time I
looked into your wild blue eyes full of hope and
wonder, I understood just how deeply I must have
hurt her, knowing she could not hold me or
comfort me. I wanted to thank her, to let her know
I was a survivor. Maybe that was genetic?

I found her. I have enclosed our letters of
correspondence so you will be able to understand
why I have kept this a secret from you all these
years. There will be things you will learn that will
slam shut doors and open new, scary ones. She
and I met and found that family is the tie that
binds, or in our case, a bind with morbid ties.
~Mom

Lowe remembered all her mother's cryptic messages. Notes were in bottles, others taped on her mom's abstract paintings. The letters all seemed to appear with forethought as if her mother were always two steps ahead of her own. They were her mother's way of communicating deeply and connecting her phantom existence with she and her father.

Lowe folded the letter back to its original form. She moved to an old wooden chair with a cold tin seat that had been her mother's thinking spot. The opened black box set at Lowe's feet, a dog just fed; content and full. Lowe just stared at it as if it would speak. She reached for the heavy box. Its sturdiness gave gravity to all that it was holding. Lowe knew her mother had an order about things. Everything inside was stacked with purpose. Lowe took the letters off the top that were wrapped in baby pink ribbon. She held the letters in her hands just feeling her body wiggle with electricity from their energy. With respect, she slid the ribbon off, opening her mother's hallowed history with reverence.

Dear Mother

Dear Mother,

When fall skips over winter and moves straight into spring, I feel cheated. I didn't get a moment to even know winter. I have to imagine and posture all the ways it must have felt. I care about winter so much because I need its comfort, it is unconditional in its support, unlike summer. Summer and I got along just fine before MS. Summer became cruel and unforgiving. We are now estranged and that's ok. I got to know summer, embrace it in the formative years when it taunted with the promise of growth and fun. Winter was always the reprieve, the exhale.

My mother was winter and my father summer. I found out I was adopted when I was a teenager and discovered I had MS. I suppose they decided that the double edged sword approach would be the swiftest way to rip off that band aid. I was angry and hurt with my parents that they were not strong enough to tell me early in my life about my being adopted. I questioned so much of our differences in appearance and behavior. My father was schizophrenic and my mother was trapped. I was her only solace even though I got to wear the shackles, too. Regardless, I loved them. I knew I had things to teach them. I've always had perspective. I knew my genetics were stronger than both of them. I tell you these things because I want you to know I never felt abandoned by you. I felt like your boomerang. I know my life has a circular trajectory.

My childhood was chaotic. It taught me to be a survivor. I am better for it. I have a daughter now. When she was born, I began to wonder about you. I have always had a sense of you. I don't mean your physical appearance. I am connected to you because I am a part of you, came from you.

My daughter and I have that same knowing. I am curious about the circumstances surrounding your decision to give me up for adoption. I don't judge you, I haven't done saintly things in my own life. I've crawled with criminals. I think I know your reasons inherently. A child that grows in a womb internalizes so much of her mother's emotion and mental jargon in that gestation period.

When I found out I was adopted, I went snooping through my mother's personal places. I knew she was hiding something. I found in her belongings a small wooden box. Inside was a key necklace with my birthdate engraved on it and a photo of you holding me. It was an old, grainy photo and you were looking down at me in profile wearing that key necklace. I put that necklace on and I never took it off. My mother knew I found the box. We never spoke of it. I vowed that one day our paths would cross. I never could have imagined how and why.

I would love to know you. ~Gabrielle Vansant

<u>Dearest Daughter</u>

Dear Child,

I was fifteen and smitten. He was my math tutor. He had auburn hair and deep dimples that I couldn't resist. He was charming, smart, and ten years older than me. When I found out I was pregnant, he advised me to get an abortion, offered to pay for it. A week after revealing my pregnancy to him, he died in a motorcycle crash. I knew I couldn't abort you. You now had purpose. I hid my pregnancy from everyone, except my sister. She was my savior. My parents were hard working and Catholic. I would never hear the end of how this child was my penance and they would have sent me off to a convent for nine long, agonizing months of guilt.

Angels appear precisely. I met your mother. She worked at the doctor's office I visited late in my pregnancy. She knew my circumstances. She offered to adopt you. She became part of your purpose. Your mother took that picture of you and me. She was sincere in regards to my feelings for you. She was always supposed to be your mother. I asked her to please give you the box when she felt it was the right time. Seems the box had legs and it found you first.

I was a detective most of my life. You have no siblings. I married once, but we were both married to our jobs so it didn't last. My career was my partner. It was rich and unconditional in the ways it loved me. I retired and I now do more intuitive detective work with those gifts of knowing we seem to have in common. Life has dealt you many gifts and I am glad that you have been able to recognize them. How could you not be so attuned? I'm glad to know you don't harbor anger toward being adopted. I did it because I had no support at the time. I was too young. I have always had a sense of you in all I ever did. You don't create life and then it magically disappears with a new family. What you create is yours forever.

About those gifts. I'm sorry our souls had to meet for the first time in a really horrible way. I can speak candidly with you about the car crash – it is what it is. I saw you checking my sister and me at that car wreck back in 1995. We were both dead. Yet, I watched you from a weird limbo between life and death. You transcended your own body in those moments, blending our shared pieces in an unspoken language, volleyed the power of love. I'm sorry we crashed into each other that way, but it was supposed to be. I knew you were my daughter as you clasped your own necklace and mine dangled awkwardly around my bloody, mangled neck. I heard you say you'd get help - it echoed. I saw you running back to your car in devastated tears. I was your pain. My soul, your soul. We were the same. I miraculously survived. So you are a survivor for a reason.

My head couldn't remember all the events of that tragic day for a long, long time. The detective in me didn't put together the trail of death until it was so very close. That experience changed me forever. Not always in good ways, I've had my share of crawling as well. I believe we are meant to know each other if only for some sort of resolution or validation? Of course, I would love to know you as well.

~ Birth Mother

Lowe felt disconnected from her body as if she were watching her life from that same bubble above. Words echoed as if lingering in the air for permanence. It was like dying and hearing your thoughts outside your physicality. Parts of Lowe were dying while depths she didn't understand were bubbling new.

Lowe folded the letters with delicate care, sliding them back into their envelopes like crumbly paper machete. Enough for one lifetime, much less a day. Her mother had always known how to drop bombs like fragile eggs. After reading the birth mother's letter, Lowe realized that dynamite was not only explosive, but genetic. This birth mother was a whole new dimension to her own mother's many faces. Since Lowe knew her mother was usually a few steps ahead, she felt certain she had already crossed paths with this birth mother. Lowe sensed a strange electricity tickling the pit of her stomach.

Dearest Lowe,

When I was first diagnosed with MS, I fell fanatical with controls. I needed things I could manipulate as my body spun wildly into a foreign orbit. I wish you had the chance to grow up in a close neighborhood like mine. That world was knit differently than now. Those neighbor kids my parents left this beach house you now call home were my world. It was a Holden, Rory, Gabby neighborhood trio. We all created monsters and

dragons to slay. I suppose we were preparing
ourselves for the storms in our lives. I had my
share and I caused a lot of storms in theirs when I
was about your age. They fell in love and I fell ill
– very different paths.

That neighborhood best friend, she had a
brother with all that control. I had a father with a
wealth of monetary information. So, I sold it to
this powerful man in exchange for escaping my
unhealthy life. This man turned out to be Madison
Peacock's first husband, Rhett. Ironically, he
turned out to be one of the unhealthiest
relationships I could have ever chosen, but my
savior from that life. He was a snake wearing
Armani. Madison was the real deal in all of this.
She saved everyone - but herself. Madison is the
true tragic heroin. She is why we bought the house
back for you. She is a buoy for our world
connected to us in cosmic ways. ~Mom

Dear Lowe,

I wish I had known you when I was a young girl. You would have been my best friend. We could have had some adventures together. I think you would have protected me from myself. I was a child that acted out whatever ate at me. I didn't pass that angst on until I was older and found out I had a disease. The gift was that it taught me how to channel my rage, sadness, perspective. Nobody will understand you fully. Only you. Never let someone make you believe they do because they can only empathize. The worst use it against you by stealing the honesty you gave them and making it their power over you. I can see your red head shaking no defiantly. But, it can happen subtly and when you finally see it for what it is, it is too late.

Kids do stupid things. They make childish mistakes that usually cost them wounded pride or embarrassment. I made some great friends as a child. I loved them like the siblings I never had. I was the queen of the trio. This shouldn't surprise or shock you in the least. I ruled the playground with my games and stories. They were such wonderfully willing participants. I don't know how they stood me most of the time. They being Rory and Holden. They were my street buddies that met up with me every afternoon to play or share the revelations of the day. We were friends until college. The two of them were hot and heavy into each other when we were teenagers. They were terrible actors, couldn't hide it well, but they tried and I appeased them. Rory was my best friend. I told her everything. Everything except that I had a crush on her big brother, Rhett Peacock. Yes, you've connected the dots. Rhett is Madison's first husband. But, I knew him first from my childhood. He didn't meet Madison until much later in his life.

Rhett helped me fake my own death to save me from my delusional father. But, it cost me my friends. Rory and Holden had bad timing and were tangled in the mess. The budding romance they planned was derailed for twenty years. Holden and Rory moved on with their life and have never truly understood my plight. That is water under the bridge now because all I care about is that everyone is living and moving forward and is safe. My young dating career ended. I was twenty with MS and on the run. Then I find out I am pregnant with you. I devoted myself to staying safe and raising you from a distance with your father's help. A strange sort of distance I never chose and I know you found hard to understand. You all will understand this distance and its relevance. It was in this time I met Madison. Madison took good care of you and me, helped raise you, all the while married to Rhett. She has always protected things for me.

The only sense of safety I ever felt in my entire life was at that beach house you now call home. My bedroom was my castle turret and I ruled, untouchable. I created some of the most

amazing stories in that room. Very heartfelt things
happened in that space you call yours. They live
on there, breathe life into all who dare to listen.
Most cannot see with eyes that don't judge in some
fashion. I have learned that the third eye is the
only one that can. I accept that as a cosmic gift
for all the heartbreak I have experienced in my
life. I hope you can see with that same eye. It will
make your world a lot less lonely even if you find
yourself isolated. I have lived a life of hibernation
and isolation the past 30 years. In all that time,
I've learned how to navigate and befriend the
demons that try to dash the hope I keep guarded
closely to my chest. Yes, demons exist. They can
be long dead and still wiggle your controls. We
never forget the impact someone has on our well
being, good or bad. ~Mom

Hannah set the letters back on Gabby's
desk. She hadn't snooped. The letter had been
sitting on the desk, opened when she bounded in

after school with her homework. It had commanded her attention, insistent she read it. The guilt was there, it brimmed in her curiosity. It enticed Hannah just as the black box had done Lowe days earlier.

The light and shadows from the sand people below danced through the window. Hannah noticed a boy running in circles around his dog. Hannah thought now that her own mother was mysterious when viewed through the eyes of a peer. This friend knew her mother differently, wrote about the other life and Madison's first husband. Hannah wondered about this Armani man who had been married to her mother so long ago. She could only remember fragments and flashes. Was this Rhett the man in her dreams? Half the memories she had chalked up to make believe. Especially the disturbing ones. No one talked much about that life in Little Rock.

Sister Friend

Lowe rapped on the door, coke in hand for Hannah. She noticed the letter on the desk and shame in Hannah's gaze. Lowe knew Hannah had confession on her mind. Hannah was walking guilt.

"What's so heavy?" Lowe handed the drink to Hannah.

"I read the letter sitting here. I know it was wrong – but – it's like they talked." Hannah didn't want Lowe to think she couldn't be trusted.

"It's OK, Hannah. I understand what you mean." Lowe smiled, easing the angst on Hannah's brow. Lowe had become Hannah's sister friend and she didn't want to compromise that friendship.

"It just said stuff in it about my mom." Hannah seemed disappointed that there were no deep, seedy secrets. But, she sensed there were bad things from her memories. Hannah stared at the floor, her eyes someplace far off. Lowe knew she was remembering disturbing events from her childhood life in Little Rock. Things she didn't understand. It had become apparent to Lowe that secrets were a normal part of Hannah's youth. Hannah was desensitized to danger. That scared Lowe.

"Hannah, I'm going to share something with you." Lowe watched the light return to Hannah's eyes. Lowe and Hannah just seemed to get each other.

"Remember that metal box we found under the boards that day? Inside the box were letters from my mother. Letters with secrets she is revealing to me – to us all." Hannah's blue eyes widened with intrigue.

"Wow, our mom's are mysterious." Hannah burped the Coca Cola with bravado.

"I kind of think most moms are. My mom does everything for a reason. That is why I'd like to share them with you." Lowe locked the door and pulled out the huge metal box. She handed the letters to Hannah to read later, privately.

An old cigar box was the next order of business. Lowe opened the dusty lid. Inside were old photos in two small sandwich zip bags. In one bag were old, square photos with white borders. The other bag held polaroid photos from the early eighties, instant technology. The polaroid photos were newer. People were more recognizable.

"These photos are so 1980's." Hannah laughed at the spiked hair and shoulder pads. Who were these style icons?

"That is my mom and her friends from childhood." Lowe flipped the polaroid over and there were names written on it.

"Holden, Rory, Rhett, Gabby." Lowe spoke their names aloud and the lights in the room seemed to buzz and hum. The photo was a story. Rhett had his arms around Rory and Gabby, smiling an arrogant grin while Holden almost clinched his teeth through his parallel smile.

"Holden and Rory are my mom's childhood friends. Rhett is Rory's older brother." Lowe confirmed the facts she knew as she watched Hannah's face sink.

"Rhett Peacock? That's my mom's first husband. He is the Armani man I see in those weird flashbacks." Hannah's pallor was splintered. Lowe flipped to the older photos quickly.

"The square ones are the oldest." Lowe stared at each photo, turning them over to see if these people were listed.

"Who are they?" Hannah reveled in decoding.

"It's my grandparents. This must be the day they adopted my mom." In Gabby's cursive it read Lexie and John Vansant. Gabby was just a baby and they were young, proud new parents.

"Your mom was adopted? Huh?" Hannah clutched the letters Lowe had given her.

"You'll know everything soon." Lowe handed Hannah a few more pictures.

"Who's that chic?" Hannah had flipped the photo, but there was nothing on the back to identify the woman.

Hannah handed to picture to Lowe. It was a young teenage girl holding Lowe's mother as a baby. She was in profile, looking stoically as baby Gabby slept.

"I'm not sure." Lowe's stomach fluttered with that soft, fuzzy electricity.

Lowe noticed a necklace around this young woman's neck that was exactly like the one her mother wore all her life. It was a unique heart shaped key. Lowe remained silent, slipping the photos back into the bag.

How do you determine the weight of words unspoken? Something new had instantly formed. Maybe it was Gabby's room. It was a treasure chest. It had some mystical energy that bonded people that had shared things in its space. Lowe and Hannah began connecting bizarre dots in a matrix they couldn't see until now. Their families were connected just enough that they didn't notice the symmetry, hadn't put their pieces of the puzzle into view. For now, they held onto their piece until the picture was clearer.

M listened from the porch to their girlish banter rise in shrill waves off the high a-framed ceiling and through the crags of the old windows. She couldn't help but smile and think of her own sister she had gaggled with so long, long ago.

Mother's Day Invitation

Mother's Day was a strange day. It bled the energies of all Mothers present and past, combining to form a mass of heartfelt oxygenated air that everyone collectively breathed. It was a moment to pay homage to the woman who gave birth to you whether she was a good or a bad mother, or even a mother at all to you. For mothers were vessels to the life you were given.

Lowe and Hannah had been secretly reading all the letters Gabby had left. It shaded their mothers in a different light. Both mothers were totally different people with their plights, flaws, and bad decisions.

Lowe understood her mother more while Hannah questioned her mother's old ways.

Lowe hadn't been able get the image of that young woman with the necklace like her mother's out of her mind. There was something emotional with the facts that Lowe couldn't ignore. She couldn't shake the pull to her. It ate at her with its familiarity. Her mother was a precise and calculated storyteller. Her mother was also very tight lipped about her past and her life. She was selective with the things she shared – especially what mattered. It was in these strange moments that Lowe realized the lady in the photo was M – Gabby's birth mother, Lowe's grandmother.

M's door was cracked slightly. The sound of the shower could be heard as the scent of her lavender shampoo danced into the hall. Lowe was off to work, but had a Mother's Day card for M.

She stepped into the room, noticing M's bag packed along with her briefcase. On top of briefcase was the file M was working on, why she was going back to Little Rock for a while.

Lowe heard M shutting off the water. She placed the Mother's Day card on the nightstand when she noticed the necklace lying beside M's watch and rings. She'd never seen M wear it. Lowe held the necklace to the window light. Her proof. Strange tears of joy began to well up in Lowe's eyes.

M sensed another body in her space. She called out to the gravity in the room, but the gravity was mum. Lowe swiftly placed the card on the nightstand, draping the necklace across it before tiptoeing out the door. M poked her head around the bathroom door, perusing the contents of the room. M smelled Lowe's perfume fading as if she had just disappeared into thin air. On the nightstand there was a bright yellow card that had simply M written on it and the necklace Lowe had

placed carefully upon it. More of an invitation
than a Happy Mother's Day. M smiled. She
finally had a granddaughter.

Hannah Beth Who?

Hannah read the letters. She confided in
Lowe that they were giving her tons of flashbacks.
Her life with Madison as her mom had seemed
well adjusted. Something was fickle with the math.
Hannah remembered Armani man. She could hear
his voice in her head. He was real as a whisper in
her ear that startled her with a soothing sort of
threat. He told her bad things about her mother that
she unconsciously brushed off because her mother,
Madison, was her savior. Hannah started
wondering if this man had been talking about her
first mother who had died? Why did she know the
things she heard? How could she remember such?

Hannah had her own Mother's Day card
planned for Madison and Dyer. It was more
inquisitive and not as loving as Lowe's was to M.

She wrote them a note that would totally open up and change Dyer and Madison's relationship with their daughter.

Dear Mom and Dad,

Some of my first memories were Dad and I going to see Mom at her office. I didn't realize we were there for counseling. Mom, you made it so easy, like a picnic every Thursday at your office. Dad was so happy to go see you. He always spiffed up and put on cologne. He loved you from the first visit. I know you have always said the lives you had before becoming my parents were rough and unhappy. I am forever grateful you adopted and loved me.

Don't freak out and send me to counseling. There are things from your other lives I am remembering. Things I think only you can answer. I don't want you to lie to me or hide your past from me. I might have only been five when you adopted me, but I saw a lot and heard a lot I now understand better.

I remember Mom's first husband. He was in the hospital very sick. He was not a nice person, had "changed" I heard you say. I heard him say mean things to Mom, threats. One time I snuck in his room when you and dad were arguing in the hallway. I walked up to his bed while he was sleeping and just stared at him. His eyes were closed and he said that I was HIS. He whispered my momma did bad, bad things. He talked low and fast about how the real me would come out someday in my DNA. His eyes popped open and he told me I would never be able to forget his eyes. He was crazy talking and scared me, so I ran out of the room. I tried to forget that. But, he was right. It came back to me in flashes. I've never forgotten him.

Lowe and I have been reading letters that her mother, Gabby left for her. Gabby is revealing her life to Lowe. These letters have pictures and *tell a story of her life and your life. There are pictures of her neighborhood friends and your first husband was in them as well. I want to know more.*

Can you please tell me the story of your life in Little Rock? The one we never speak about. I want to know where I came from before I was five.
~Hannah

DNA Don't

Hannah's letter was no surprise to Dyer or Madison. Every teenager begins that journey of self-exploration much further than their own backyard. They long to know how they fit into the fabric of their parent's lives as well as this large, vast world that seemed to have everything to offer. Choices are power and the world is at their feet for a small time.

Giving up ghosts means embracing them, owning them. Ghosts haunt if they aren't befriended with honesty; their purpose to remind us how we got to be the people we are now. How Dyer and Madison reveal Hannah's roots will define how she deals with the reality. Dyer and Madison found they weren't quite as ready as they thought.

Ever since Rhett's death and the trauma back in 2007, Hannah had trouble connecting her emotions with the actions happening around her. She had learned to view her trauma through others' reactions. Others that were good at wearing masks.

Dyer and Madison were both very different people back in 2007. They learned that reacting or not reacting were essentially the same thing. The only difference was how the outcome appeared to the onlooker. The onlooker being Hannah Beth. Dyer and Madison had been very passive aggressive, playing down the gravity of the nightmare they were enduring at the time. They feverishly tried to put Hannah in that protective bubble of innocence, knowing no human can shun the vibes of others, particularly children.

The weather was pithy, almost whiny gusts that rattled the windows like a screaming toddler. Tears brimmed, a quiet waterfall down Madison's cheeks. The day had finally come. Dyer laced his fingers into hers and ushered them out the door and onto the sand. The wind a bouncy ball of energy this late spring day, volatile as the lumps in their throats they fought. They walked in silence at first, letting the ocean tides usher in their words.

"Hannah's going to hurt us with this. We have to do this together." Dyer wasn't afraid of losing his daughter as he had been so many years ago. That threat seemed irrelevant.

"She's brooding and I just can't…can't relive this without you." Dyer could only see the fine line of Madison's lips moving as she spoke. Her hair camouflaged the rest of her face.

"Why now?" Dyer rubbed the back of his neck with his callused hand, his anxiety matching Madison's.

"I've wondered the same thing." Madison's stared at Dyer with a glint of faith and a lot of gravity and doom.

They made their way back to the house and found Hannah sitting on the porch. She was ready to talk. Madison looked at her daughter with humbled, pensive eyes. Dyer kept his hands in his pant pockets. Caution perched around the corners of Hannah's mouth. Her face pleaded guilty, masking her tension. She was a child in a grown-up body that still needed rules for her sharp tongue. They were about to change her life forever.

"Sounds like we need to talk." Madison broke the humid air with motherly authority. Dyer put his arm around his daughter, sadly sensing her innocence slipping from his fingers.

"Where do we begin?" Madison clinched her left fist, prepared to punch the past into submission.

"I just remember these voices I can't place. Faces I don't think I was supposed to see or know. It just feels weird. I feel conflicted." Hannah's blue eyes were in moments that frightened her, sending her to strange child-like gazes that they all understood too well.

"I thought you figured these out with counseling?" Madison knew some repressed thoughts would arise again.

"The man you were married to before...was he famous?" Hannah had cooled her guilt and revved up the sass, unsure of what to ask her mother about this strange subject.

Dyer watched Madison go rigid. Dyer intercepted this question.

"His name was Rhett Peacock. He was a lawyer. I would say he was infamous, bad." Dyer put his arm around Madison and took over.

"So, why did you stay with him if he was so bad? Was he rich? Daddy why did we stay and not just take Mom away?" Hannah's rage she hadn't processed had been buried since she was six. It cleverly began to slip in moody bursts.

Hannah's eyes went to places Dyer and Madison both understood.

"Hannah, why are you opening this can of worms now?" Dyer sensed more fueling his daughter's sudden interest.

Hannah didn't flinch, reeled in her mania and inquired as if she were a hot headed reporter. She was tired of feeling torn.

"I read all these letters about Mom and Rhett. All these secrets both of you have hidden from me." There was judgment in his daughter's smarmy posture that felt genetic.

"They were your very bad DNA. That is why we hid them. The fact you are having these feelings is proof why." Madison tone was flat, honest. She didn't admit to anything, yet she admitted everything.

"That is not an answer! That's just counseling! That's not fair!" Hannah's blue eyes raged as she crossed her arms, sullen.

"I was married to Rhett Peacock for all the wrong reasons. I found you, kept you away from him, for good ones. It wasn't your life, it was mine. That's all you're going to get for now." Madison stood up to Hannah with authority that startled her daughter. Madison was tired of breathing this toxic air surrounding Rhett.

Madison strode into the house, slamming the door and rattling the windowpanes. Hannah looked to Dyer, tears in her bulging eyes.

"Don't make your mother get fiery. You'll always lose. Is this really coming from just the letters?" Dyer always had the sixth sense regarding his daughter.

"Lowe told me Momma knows Gabby from way back. Gabby's letters talked about Momma and Rhett. Gabby made Rhett sound like some god to fear. The letters made me remember when we lived in Little Rock. They made me wonder why I feel such fear from back then. Things don't add up." Hannah rocked back and forth in the glider, pulling her long legs to her chest.

"Rhett was not any sort of god. You'll never know what hell your momma and I went through. You aren't supposed to know everything. You'll know what you need in the right time." Dyer watched Hannah connect his simple formula. She smiled.

"I didn't mean to hurt you." Hannah wiped her moody tears. Preteen tears she often didn't understand.

"Yes, you did, Hannah." Dyer spoke from his own angst. He knew Hannah would always hurt or wound others from those scars from her brief life in Little Rock.

"Was that Madison Peacock I read about in the letters the same one back in Little Rock?" Hannah had intrigue, yearning in her tone.

"That Madison Peacock wasn't easy to love and hard to know. Life made her careful, private. She's not perfect or all good. She saved your life once." Dyer stood, rubbing his formidable daughter's shoulder.

"I guess I wanted to know her like in the letters." Hannah smiled at the man who always knew how to make her feel understood.

"You know her. You are the one thing she never wanted to leave or let down." Dyer's words redirected to the door.

The screen creaked open as Madison reappeared, calmed. Hannah looked to her mother with fresh eyes.

"Everyone has secrets. We don't want to show the mistakes, just the hard earned lessons." Madison's eyes weren't angry, but firm in her truth.

"Just say it, tell me - please, Mom."
Hannah had to hear it from her mother's mouth -
what she suspected all along.

"Rhett Peacock is your biological father."
Madison had put it out into the wicked air that
swirled the beach that afternoon. What the wind
would do with it was its business. What Hannah
would do with this information was her choice.

The In Between

The house was maudlin, whining colors and
textures past, a time machine of frozen unkempt
emotion. It spoke from a time that was once safe,
a comfortable place for a child to grow up. This
childhood home had Madison feeling like the one
left behind.

Marcella turned to her daughter. Marcella
was young, still a dreamer. She was wearing a
vintage 80's blouse with giant shoulder pads that
puckered in places, making a "woman power"
statement. She was holding up black and red bits

of wallpaper samples to the faded green and mauve walls.

"This paper is old and morbid. I think it's time for something new." Marcella held the fabrics high, eyeballing each choice. The dated house sickened like freak show mirrors that deceived the balance.

"Wallpaper is just awful, Mom. Paper isn't for walls." There was a weird dissidence that saturated Madison with confusion. This scene was paradox.

"Walls are walls no matter how you dress them." Suddenly, those walls faded. Words never seemed spoken, just understood in this odd wrinkle of time.

Madison was now driving her mother's Oldsmobile. It was night, raining in bursts and sheets and Madison couldn't see the knob to turn on the headlights. Her vision was failing, fuzzy, begging bifocals. She stomped the brake and the bloated body style of the Oldsmobile only fishtailed worse. Momentum seized the car's control as Madison navigated an abrupt corner. The steering wheel possessed in a peculiar polar opposition. Madison focused on the horizon, decelerating as best she could, hugging the edge of all uncertainty.

"Stop fighting this, Madison. You're making it too hard." Marcella was now in the passenger's seat. She seemed pensive and frustrated with the dreamer.

"But, I can't find the lights, Mom!" Madison looked down at the steering wheel and she saw her mother's hands holding the wheel, postured as she always had, assuredly one palm somewhere between northeast and the other somewhere between northwest.

"You're not really wanting to see the light, are you? If you were, it would find you." Madison let go of the steering wheel. Marcella disappeared from the car.

The car flew off the road, high into the air, and Madison held her breath, feeling her mother's anxiety as it rushed her body. She fell to the earth like lead with such force that it killed the engine, totally stopping the momentum, unlike the end over end wreck that had killed her mother. This collision was obtuse in its teaching. Madison sat in the steel Oldsmobile, unscathed, and started to cry at the irony.

"You were murdered, weren't you, Mom?" Madison's chest ached when she finally acknowledged her mom's code.

"It took you long enough." Marcella stood smiling at Madison through the driver's window that was now frosty and sentimental.

"But I don't want this knowledge...I miss you." Madison put her palm to the window as if she could touch her mother's smile.

"You're my good girl. I really hate it that I am dead. Find the light, Madison." Marcella winked at her daughter with a wry grin in affirmation.

"I'll find them, Mom." Madison mumbled audibly, waking Dyer.

August 2015

Not So Deaf Ears

Madison and Dyer awoke most mornings to children's shrill screams, boisterous thumps, and moody banter. Mix teenagers and toddlers and you get drama. This morning was no different as the very mundane, quiet adult day gave way to the roar of normal.

Dyer thought the letter was unassuming. It looked like most mail in a manila envelope. Dyer's eyes welled up with tears, his fists angry mallets, denting the kitchen countertop.

Inside were photographs of Dyer's first wife, freshly dead on the floor in their bathroom. Particularly morbid as if taken when she had just died. As he thumbed through the photographs, he noticed they seemed to chronicle his life from his wife's death to exact moments just days ago. There was no note, nothing but photos that told their own timeline and highlighted crimes and atrocities no one should know. It brought Dyer

Brown to his knees and back into a past that therapy would only vex.

Madison gathered her mail at the hospital and retired to her office for lunch. The manila envelope nauseated Madison with photos of her mother and aunt at the scene of their crash twenty years ago. Her mother brutally mangled and nearly decapitated. Her aunt a rag doll, twisted and bloated with swelling and bruising, unrecognizable. The most chilling photo was one of Houston lying face first in the sand after his death. He was blue and obviously freshly deceased. On the back of each photo, it read MURDERED. These pictures were not taken by police or investigators. Madison stuffed the photos back into the envelope, realizing her dreams were now her only safe place. She reached for her cell phone and dialed M.

The chatter of living in a household becomes a theme song. It seeps into the walls and carpet like odor and memory. It reminds us of times we wished walls could talk and take us to magical conversations with our childhood. It also cautions us that no matter, words permeate places forever. They scar solace, maim perceptions, build character into the structures they possess. Like the fine lines of wisdom on a beautiful smile, they charm. Most things uttered or spoken weren't filtered or carefully considered when in our safe places. When Madison and M had conversations, the walls seemed to perk up and began to listen to what was not being said.

The Capital Hotel

M paced the veranda square, looking down upon the guests in the lobby, moving in and out like ants under an August magnifying glass. The concierge wore sweat like a wrist watch. He greeted people in the August Arkansas summer heat and humidity with a shiny face and a docile smile. M observed families bounding in from the day's vacation activities, the parents zombies, the children electric and loud.

M began to think that innocence was overrated, oblivion not protection. Her view highly biased and profound she surmised. She wished she could give the obtuse her super powers for just a day. She knew that idea would never work. Life is a hard earned love affair. Using your powers for the good doesn't produce easy, quick results. Complacency or taking the easy route is usually the most painful stake a person could choose. Not listening to one's life was one giant head butt over and over again.

A mother and daughter embraced. The mother much slighter than her daughter, yet strong and protective. She cradled her daughter's head on her shoulder, rubbing her back as the daughter obviously was crying. M watched this scene with remorse. She had never been a matriarch to Gabby or even to Madison after the death of her mother. It seemed like a foreign role she had never assumed. Mothers release their young to fly on their own, forge their identity. M had never had the opportunity to establish bonds, so she never felt entitled to those emotions. Huge tears streamed down M's cheeks. For the first time, she thought of Gabby and Madison as her own. The eminent threat that lingered around both of them now had stirred a very pointed protectiveness she had never quite sharpened to a fine a point as she had now. God had right timing and she believed in it more now than ever.

M stared down at the smarmy devil who had cowardly eluded her for too long. He wore his hair short and spiked and he was leaner now, more rugged like the person's life he had stolen. M suspected he had taken that life for his own, but he was too clever for that to ever be proven. He had altered his face with surgery, but the eyes never lied. He sat reading the newspaper, looking at his expensive watch numerous times. A petite woman with jet black salt and pepper hair approached him.

She sauntered the same as M had remembered, the salt in her prickly hair more for show. She had work done, a nose job, work on her cheeks. Her lips still pouty and full, upturned by a surgeon. The dark brown eyes filled with consummate guilt had always branded her crazy like a fox. They hugged and kissed and M felt her stomach knot into balls of betrayal. She knew narcissism like theirs couldn't be understood with rational compassion and empathy. She didn't even want to try. M had fallen on that double edged sword many a midnight hour and it only led her to dark and seething thoughts.

A hand grazed M's shoulder, a leaf in a fall breeze – subtle and startling – before it rested gently, wrapping it's skinny, crooked fingers into her own.

"That is disgusting and disconcerting." Gabby wore tortoise horn rimmed glasses, her chestnut red hair now cut in a funky, artsy bob.

Streaks of gray or platinum stood out in her temples.

"That is why we are here. We've finally got him." M liked the feel of her daughter's hand in hers. M pulled Gabby away from the balcony view and she hugged her daughter the way that mother had done just moments earlier.

"Lowe knows I'm her grandmother. She and Hannah have read your letters." Gabby laid her head on M's shoulder, nestled into the nape of M's neck as if it were made just for her. There was pause, still as their hearts beat in unison, a child in her mother's womb.

"We are all family - finally." Gabby spoke from behind her walls of hurt all those years.

"It's time to share everything with our family." In this safe pause, they shared the unconditional. It had no words, just warmth and peace.

M's cell phone vibrated in her pocket. It was Madison calling. M showed the call to Gabby.

Just great timing. She walked to a private corner where she could be unheard.

"Dyer and I got brutal, crime scene type photos in the mail today. Rhett is alive, isn't he?" Madison didn't even say hello. Her breathing metered and fraught with fear.

"Yes, dear. I'm sending you a video." M looked down at the imposter and his dutiful mistress. M knew Rhett was closing in on them all. The sense of righting wrongs she had always known crept up her spine in a slow tickle.

Interrogation of Lane Godair

As interrogations went, this one was no different. Small room with a table where the detective faced the person being questioned. The conversation was videoed. Lane sat stoically, awaiting M's arrival. She sipped on a bottled water very gingerly and with restraint.

M opened the door swiftly and with purpose. Lane peered at the table, M at her notes.

It was an odd attempt at objectivity. M knew all about Lane's history with Madison and Rhett.

"You are Lane Godair, correct?" M glanced up at Lane with a quick complacent grin. Her salt and pepper hair complimented her smile.

"Yes." Lane nervously put her hands in her lap, unsure of how to posture.

"How did you know Rhett Peacock?" M always cut to the guts.

"He was my employer. I was a lawyer in his law firm." Lane tilted her head sideways as if ushering more.

"What about Madison Peacock? How do you know her?" M tilted her head as well, mimicking Lane.

"I worked with Madison at Rhett's law firm. They were married. She was my friend." Lane chose her words like a picky eater. Friend would be the last word M would have chosen.

"Who is this person?" M slid a photo of Hannah Beth Brown in front of Lane. Guilt crept up into Lane's posture.

"Hannah Brown. That is Madison's daughter. She's my biological daughter." Lane didn't flinch.

"Is Rhett her biological father?" Lane shifted in her chair. Merely hot coals.

"Yes." Lane was used to being a very numb lawyer.

"Ms. Godair, do you know why you are here?" M could hear the lights buzzing overhead. It was a heavenly hum.

"No." Lane stared down M with wide eyes. Aloof was safe.

"Rhett Peacock died back in 2007. We have reason to believe he faked his death and quite possibly assumed a new identity." M pulled out a series of photos and laid them on the desk in front of her, one by one.

"You know these people well. They all have one thing in common." M watched Lane study the photos, acting almost abhorred.

"These people are all connected to Rhett and Madison Peacock?" Lane pushed back subtly.

"They are all dead. Photographically captured dead by their killer." M waited for a rebuttal.

Silence.

"First, we have a photo of Dyer Brown's first wife, freshly dead. Madison's husband, Houston King, freshly dead. All of these people are tied to you just as much." M watched the perfectly smooth lines between Lane's eyes begin to furl and twitch.

"Ties don't make me a killer." Lane just peeped.

"Ties like yours to all these people make for opportunity. Dyer and his first wife adopted Hannah from you. It was long after you were friends with Madison. When Dyer's wife turned up dead, who recommended Madison for counseling – none other than you. When Madison failed to fall under your and Rhett's control, married Houston King, and had his child, you both unleashed again and had him killed." M watched Lane's neck flush crimson.

"It was Vincent Godair. He was Rhett's right hand, not me." Lane ratted out her awful genetics that should be the prime suspect.

"That's convenient considering he's dead, too, and by your hand. You're Rhett's right hand." M pushed Lane into a corner, not letting her worm her way out of any guilt.

"What in the hell would I have to gain by killing all these people?!" Lane slapped her palm firmly on the photos.

"No, my dear, it isn't what you'd gain. It is what you'd lose - which is everything." M held up the final photo. It was time stamped 2015. It showed Rhett Peacock and Lane Godair arm in arm walking though the doors of the Capital Hotel in Little Rock.

Madison closed the video and tossed her phone across the room. Rhett Peacock was enough to explain to her daughter. Lane, Hannah's biological mother, was a can of worms for another life.

Drowning in Dreams

The room was full of Rhett's distant family and business associates. A visitation of sorts. There was a yellow green tint to the light that nauseated with foreboding. The room hummed with a static sort of energy that bordered menacing. Everyone seemed to pack their rage behind placid smiles. It was exhausting and was giving Madison a headache, her eyes squinted to minimize the noxious light.

"Light shouldn't be toxic." A voice from behind Madison echoed off her eardrums, more rooted in her soul than the room.

Madison turned around and the floor gave way to rushing water, plunging the voice into the water. Madison watched this blur of color struggle with outstretched arms deep under the surface of the water's clarity. None of the placidity in the room skipped a beat as people kindly ignored and overlooked the drowning occurring around them.

"Don't fight the water. Let go and float. I'll get you." Madison knelt at the water's edge, whispering to the figure her promises, fixated on how the trapped voice began to buoy.

Madison waited and when she felt she could reach the arms she saw flailing, she bent over into the water up to her elbows, snatching the wrists and pulling this woman out of the water with the fluidity of childbirth. The woman wrapped her arms and legs around Madison, limp and tired as a newborn. Madison stepped far away from the water's edge. No one turned to help. No one even idled their agendas for this woman. Madison felt a calculation in the room that bested her heartfelt intentions.

Madison laid the woman on the ground, gently cradling her head and neck. She brushed the long, brown hair away from the voice's face to find that the woman was her mother. Long, deep seated sobs grew in Madison's baritone. Her chest hadn't the capacity to emote the weight and enormity of her discovery; longing was wrapped around everything Madison did or tried to become. Madison noticed the room grow darker, ominous. The family faces once smiling were turning sinister and robotic.

"You saved the parts of me that mattered. You chose wisely." The voice emanated from this flat darkness.

Quick, pinpoint pops could be heard in the next room, followed with weighted thumps of gravity. Madison knew guns with silencers. She hit the ground as Rhett's family and friends, who were supposed to love and respect on another, began picking each other off in a show of power and dominance. Madison crawled through the carnage, realizing her mother was just another one of the casualties of Rhett's war.

The next dream bled into the other with a forceful similarity that tasted bitter. The desk clock ticked in a focused, menacing alto, it's steel gear mechanism a squeaky wheel. Gabby lay on a familiar floor under a ceiling fan that whirled in a frantic, off-centered rhythm. Gabby was sprawled on the floor, her arms and legs laid out like cooked spaghetti. She began to move and gripped something in her hand. Gabby raised the right hand to her vision and found she was holding a pistol. She raised the left one and it was red as fire, stained with blood and a nasty debris that felt fleshy and sick. She could hear labored, gurgles nearby. Rhett was slumped in his large leather office chair, a hole in his chin bled copious rivers of red. The smell of leather and cigar nauseated.

"I almost got the bastard. Payback for killing your mother." Gabby was disoriented, not processing what she had just just done.

A dark police uniform walked over and stood over Gabby. It was M. Gabby looked disappointed, lunged with the gun to shoot him again, but M stopped her. M ushered Gabby out the back door as she quickly staged the scene to fit Rhett's uncle's mafia hit M.O. before the other officers arrived. M left Rhett to unsuccessfully die, trying to save her family.

Both dreams ended and blended abruptly. It slammed shut like a portal doorway to another time, leaving her with distinct and pointed feelings, smells, and colors, before morphing into something dark, yet more telling. The wall clock's second hand ticked with even purpose as Madison savored these revelations. Death was too easy for Rhett. He had to be stopped.

Dyer's foot found hers under the covers. He gently rubbed his toes over the tender top of her own as if to say good morning. It was a new day with new nightmares to navigate. The photos they had received hastened their feet with old fear. Everyone of her family had always been saving Madison. Only now, Madison had to save herself. She had no dignity left to lose, just everyone she chose to love.

Madison Peacock

I wouldn't say I am a lady, yet. That title is held by those who navigated their lives a lot more consistently. A true lady defers often, choosing her battles wisely. Guess it wasn't for my bloodline. My mother wasn't a lady, either. We have always chosen to win no matter the cost. I learned that honestly. We are both survivors. My mother had to be my father as well, so that left little time for astuteness. There is nothing noble in this because most of our survival was born of our choices. At least my mother owned her choices. I got handed a lot of things that weren't mine. Yet, I chose to try to right those wrongs out of a twisted debt to a universe that was sending things into my life I truly needed. I ignored my gifts and swam with my ego, tried to please, ate my feelings like broken glass, praying I could keep them down. I did for the longest time. I made lemonade out of the grove of lemons my associations had metastasized. There comes a point in anyone's journey where there is a lot more to lose than money, power, or things in order to finally see the beauty in concession. Walls are built to keep things out or in - shore things up when we feel compromised. These very walls act as our roadblocks as well. The shards of our living that knock our feet out from under us and force us to feel consequences.

No one truly knows me. I don't even know me. I am an image born of others' expectations. I have always bent to the will of acceptance. I've never truly taken what I wanted or made much my own unless my circumstances forced me. I am not a brave person by nature. Life has given me moxie and it can be misconstrued as bravery. I have a multitude of emotional skeletons hidden in places I'll never reveal. I'll deal with them in my own way. No one would remotely dare them.

Life has a way of self-correcting. I think the very things I gained taught me how wrong I was in my process. My daughter Hannah Beth showed me the love I had missed so much in deep ways. A love my mother had given me. Hannah was my first husband's child with another woman he used, the child merely leverage. I vowed he'd never tarnish that child the way he had me. This other woman was smart enough to give his child up for a better life, yet weak and calculating enough to hang around Rhett for the riches. Hannah was fortunate. She was adopted by the most honest man. At the time, he would call himself flawed and selfish. Dyer would give you the shirt off his back if you were cold. He was the father figure, the loving acceptance and faith I have always knew existed. I began to counsel Dyer and Hannah after Dyer's wife died. Hannah was five and without a mother. I was without love. I needed them. As a counselor, I knew the lines I shouldn't tread. Something always felt right about them. There was a faith I was supposed to know in their need. They were genuine and sincere. There was nothing normal or giving in that first marriage of mine. It was cold and self-gratifying and had nothing to do with love. How these two gifts were attained would appear convoluted and born of manipulation, when in fact it was the most honest, heartfelt desire I had ever coveted. It was my life speaking to me in the truest sense.

Rhett Peacock was my first husband and first really hard lesson. He taught me everything a man was never to be. I was young and broken, my mother was freshly dead. I needed something to fill that almost spastic emptiness. My heart was a gray crater, full of holes I desperately worked to fill. Naïve, needy, and angry at the world, I didn't notice my lure to Rhett made those caverns deeper. His charming exterior was oxymoronic. I mistook his silver tongued control of situations as love and devotion. He was smart enough to see assets in me. He loved himself. He fashioned me for what I could give him, the atrocities I could help him commit. I admit I willingly turned a blind eye just so. If you do not get an ample fill of certainties in your early life, you misconstrue truths.

It was when I finally got wise, wasn't willing or useful to him anymore, that our hating began. In Rhett's mind, assets were only valuable if they appreciated. If possible, Rhett Peacock got greedier. He jumped from one Ponzi scheme to the next bad idea until he was no longer the asset. All his evil had conspired to eradicate him, had enough of him. He was planning a faux murder, but Gabby got to him first, so his escape wasn't as he planned. That was when my true nightmare began. His evil cohorts came for their money.

Rhett absconded with what he could. His choices had been made mine, were mine now, and I had no control. I found myself shackled to these manic circumstances. My life was falling to ruin. My beautiful Hannah and Dyer were caught in the crossfire. I worked feverishly from my bully ego that was filled with terror. My choices, not Rhett's, were now affecting the very people I cherished. So, I did what I knew. I threw everyone I loved under the proverbial bus. I ran as fast and as far as I could muster.

My ability to know how to love was so damaged. I moved my feet to my safe beach. I left Dyer and Hannah in Little Rock with that other life. I thought that would save them. I didn't know how to love myself, yet they loved me anyway, stood by me even though. I felt cold. Nothing felt natural or fair. Love had equaled control in my other world. Everyone I had opened my heart to had betrayed me. I rebelled. I fist fought with all those old demons. I had so much rage it had built a wall around me. I trusted complete strangers more than those closest to me. Houston King was one of those strangers. He fell into my lap like a loaded gun. I was irrational and broken. He soldered my confidence just enough. He helped me escape Rhett. Victories were just band aids to my much bigger issues. Winners get deafened by the highs. I wasn't truly listening. I wouldn't listen for a long, long time.

I loved Dyer Brown. I had always loved Dyer in ways that I still couldn't allow myself to fully know. Chasms of emptiness left by my mother's death might seep into my heart and ambush me. Dyer was the noblest, and I didn't know how to do noble. I'm not saying he was perfect. He could be demanding, had a quick temper. He was a gentle father. He had an excellent compass.

Dyer and I bought a beach house near the one of Rhett's I sold. We were going to raise Hannah together. Then, I found out I was pregnant with Houston's son, Peck. Dyer offered to raise Peck as his own son. My life was handing me another diamond and I didn't know how to love or appreciate this trial. Old fear and self-loathing rose high in my throat. It was born of years of a rhetoric that toggled around my skull. Once again, I listened to the bombastic, not my life. I caved, moved in with Houston, another man I hardly loved, but felt I could insulate myself just so, that arm's length safe stranger. Dyer stood by my choices.

Along came my son. Peck was joy, unconditional love. He wasn't all about death. His chuckle was old and wise as his words were babyish. He taught me to see the world without many boundaries. I learned, dipped my toes into the ephemeral space inside that had been a locked door. This new focus helped me know that Houston was always merely another messenger to something more. Regrets beckoned. That life with Dyer sat an agonizing stone's throw away. I yearned for that something right about us. I cried, I physically hurt for him. I grieved for those lost and pushed away. It was in the pain that love was thrust through my heart. Agony painted the joys brighter.

Houston and I decided to go our separate ways. He knew of my feelings for Dyer. Then, Houston died. I had finally lost enough to truly win. I couldn't deny or let someone else dictate the life that was my own - ever again. I had to commandeer and navigate the emotional waters I sailed. I had to grab my gold I earned. Stacked stone by stone with all the foreign and mismatched pieces, I had constructed a tower of experience that was beautifully flawed. My bad choices were my diamonds in the rough. My story is everyone's journey, imperfectly correct. There are no wrongs, just opportunities to do right.

My aunt M re-emerged in my life with a timing that was all her own. My aunt was an intuitive. She was a natural detective. Clues always had deeper hues in her world. M never spoke of the crash that had killed my mother. It had spared her life by threads. I had assumed it was a survivor guilt she owned. When my mother died, I began dreaming of her very vividly. Dreams that I never chalked up to a much larger connection. I hadn't understood the whispers when I was grounded to my self-image. My mother was wickedly attuned to the others, throttling me with insight I only noticed in hindsight. When I allowed myself, I accepted the inevitabilities of the crash. M had supported and sheltered me twenty years, knowing my mother had been murdered. I had viewed M through the wrong lens.

The photos arrived. Photographs sent to Dyer and me separately. Grisly pictures of the freshly dead people we had lost, present and past. They were taken as proof, for a killer who was trying to send a very jealous, personal message. A very emotional threat we had seen in my other life.

Mafia calculated, a bulls-eye aimed directly at us all. There was a pathology to this method. We weren't aloof sitting ducks. This puppeteer made us knowing targets. These photos sent individually were divisive, meant to challenge our loyalty to one another. Would we share the photos with each other or would we try to hide and protect the other? This was someone who had watched us for a long, long time. The old Madison would hide and be a savior to her detriment. The old Dyer would fight unproductively and give away his power, compromising his family. This time that someone had underestimated the power of our worthiness.

The After

The ocean swayed brawny and commanding. The water rippled like a sonnet, fluid and well-versed. It had confidence in its cadence, surety in its crashing into the sand. It was almost bully, punching the sand into an odd submission that the sand understood. The push and the pull of the tides made water and sand lovers, often times enemies, but the rhythm always synched a balance at the end of the day.

Madison walked alone, listening to the story in the August tides. They had always spoken to her, always mirrored her own life and relationships. She had been introverted, the observer the past months. She didn't speak about her Mother's Day conversation with Hannah. She and Hannah had shared silent space together, spoke in coded ways mothers and daughters navigated the uncomfortable. Madison let Hannah absorb how this new found identity would shape her for the future. That was the hardest thing Madison had ever done. She knew her daughter needed space to grow. She couldn't protect her from the evil serpents that promised her shiny red fruit in exchange for parts of her dignity and heart. Madison's love was tattered, betrayed, yet it still beat with loving urgency, stronger in heart ways.

Hannah had questions at times about the paper people she now knew were three dimensional. Hannah and Lowe had been sharing a lot of their similar history. These letters that Lowe had revealed to Hannah were words that pulled the girls into their parents' novel lives.

Light rain began to fall on Madison. It refreshed her skin, left a chill to her bones as it sliced through the August humidity with precision. Something deep within Madison surfaced. It wasn't rage; it wasn't fear. It had a texture she had only known as a child. It was a form of acceptance, humility. She sat in the sand and watched the water rush her toes. She listened to the rain tap gently on her shoulders, whispers from places hidden and sacred. Madison smelled her mom's intense breath mints mingled with the salt air. Their signature potency had often passed under Madison's nose when the two were in intense conversation, seated side by side. She could see storms in the distance, lightening promised their ferocity. In that moment, she knew an odd peaceful fearlessness. Madison had revisited old dusty emotions she had buried with Rhett. Feelings she hadn't wanted to tangle. Madison knew she had to go forward and chase those storms that taunted and teased in the distance.

A creamy, lithe figure moved closer into Madison's periphery. It's sway almost a dance. It plopped its gangly legs and limbs beside Madison with a labored sigh. The rain was merely a humid mist now. Nothing was spoken as the sound of their breaths synced with the other. Madison could feel her daughter studying her, probing her deeper than the skin with that childlike fear that she had always quelled. Madison put her arm around Hannah's broad shoulder in affirmation, opening the door of dialogue between them.

"What's going on in that head of yours, Hannah Beth?" Madison saw gears turning and shifting, electrifying her light blue eyes.

"I'm not falling for that one. You're trying to analyze me." Hannah scoffed, but it was loaded with a thick need. Madison read vibes better than words.

"A mom's got to try." Madison had cooled her temper around Hannah. It had been misdirected and she recognized it. She didn't want Hannah to feel caged and unheard.

"I don't like this weirdness, Momma. It feels like I'm hurting you just being me. I'm sorry." Hannah tried to understand her mom's anger and disdain. Her youth kept her in the dark.

"Weirdness. I like that. You aren't hurting me. You're the joy. What hurts me is all the debris I thought I had managed to put away and bury with my first marriage." Madison caught a tiny shell that rolled onto her toes.

"He hurt you, does he still hurt you?" Hannah sounded thirteen going on twenty-five.

"He haunts me. Weirdness is talking to you about this. I loved him, but he wasn't capable of love. He just liked the idea of me." Madison felt her daughter's hope hanging on her words.

"So, he was retarded or wasn't all bad at first?" Hannah fished carefully.

"I know you don't want to think you've got that retarded badness in your DNA, but the truth is that we all do, are capable of evil. That's why girls like the bad boys. It seems mysterious, but it's just trouble. We have choices; we aren't programmed like your IPhone makes you think. From my experience, something hurt this man and he chose a very dark path." Madison felt Hannah's long skinny arm wrap around her waist. They sat in silence for a long while.

"You never worried about my DNA? That I might go evil or rogue?" Hannah giggled.

"Of course I did, but my lessons with dysfunction and your dad's would teach you to know yourself. We know you'll make mistakes, do crazy teenage stuff until you're twenty-five and your frontal lobes are fully developed." Madison had kidded Hannah about the lobes since puberty hit.

"God, Mom, you always shrink wrap me." Hannah shoulder-butted Madison.

"Hannah, the difference between your DNA and Rhett's is that your parents took time with you so that you would learn and own the mistakes and choices, not blame others and seek raging revenge. Dyer and I have made them all, no need to rehash them." The air between their breaths felt lighter, fluid.

"Did you know Gabby is adopted? Did you know M is her mother? That makes us all family." Hannah was fishing deeper into the family waters.

"Yes, we are all family. Do you want to know them all better?" Madison hoped she did. Gabby, Lowe, and M were welcome gifts from all of the mistakes.

"Yes. I want to know all about them – if they want to claim me." Hannah's self-esteem had taken a blow with these new genetic realities.

"M and Lowe could show you things about our family that I never could." Madison hoped that someone could give her the confidence she had always had in her daughter.

"I'd like that." Hannah seemed fascinated in the travesty that was all their stories.

"Gabby mended that fence, gave Lowe the childhood beach house. She reunited us." Madison basked in Hannah's fascination with possibilities. She missed that kind of innocence.

"Sounds like Lowe and I have super strong moms." Hannah's eyes were far away as she imagined their lives on this beach.

"Ironic, it was always the one bad string that we tried to run from that attached us all. Good always comes from the bad. If that makes us super, then so be it." Another shell rolled onto Madison's toes. Hannah snatched it this time.

"Geez, the shells love you!" Hannah examined the tightly coiled sea glass.

"They should. This beach holds so many of my secrets. You'll understand them one day. Maybe you'll share yours with the tides?" Madison fished the shell from Hannah's palm and placed it in her pocket. They both thought of Houston and his vast shell collection that still sat poignantly in their living room. A reminder of his faith in truth.

"Momma, I'm sorry for all your losses." Hannah's starry blues eyes validated and honored all those lost.

"You're a good girl, Hannah. Always look for the lights." Madison looked lovingly into Hannah's eyes and she couldn't help but think of her own mother and what she would have thought of her beautiful granddaughter.

"What does that even mean, Mom?!" Mother and daughter walked the beach hand in hand. The beach was desolate, the sand stick pins to the body.

The storms lurked in their shadows. Dyer and Peck had just abandoned a sand castle they had built only to watch a pernicious wave steal it's footing and send it back to the ocean. The duo cheered as if their favorite football team had just made a touchdown. Lowe waved from her front porch, snapping photos of the impending weather. No one but Hannah noticed the shadow figure perched high in Gabby's window.

Madison's Letter to Her Dead Husband

I don't care anymore. I really give two figs about what YOUR feelings were because it was always, always about your feelings. I watched it all my life but from a very lonely place since my mother died. I don't care about what your needs were since you never cared about my needs. It was about you – never feeling a compassionate bone in your body for others unless it was laced with motivations. Your work was the biggest albatross of mine. You always had unrealistic

ideas about how something worked.   You could
never see the large picture or how to NOT put your
cart before your horse. I tried to make our law
business successful. I invested what I could and I
watched you let me, then you coddled all the vile
thieving men around you that you doled power to
so foolishly.

Did you know I wouldn't leave or betray
you? Did you think it was out of some love or
respect that I stayed? No, because I believed in
my abilities to do right and that your underhanded
short cuts would only leave you without and never
learning lessons. I guess that it was my choice to
prove I could do it, that I am worthy and strong.
Little did I know back then that I have always been
strong. You have always been fearful and
arrogantly confident when you were truly clueless.
That was a very good manipulative way to get
others to do your bidding. I get manipulation now.
It doesn't mean I evade it. It just means that I
recognize it when it walks in and I can choose to

bow down a bit to keep peace or I can assert my power with wisdom and facts.

We appeared to have a good marriage. You provided for us and we lived a rich appearance. However, I didn't realize it until my mother died that she was the one who provided all the warm love. You were not capable of truly letting me have that part of you. I don't know what was damaged in you that you had to shut life off into your own world and color your truths with falsehoods. I really hate that you couldn't open up and be yourself – whoever that may be? You seemed to morph into whatever would get you what you needed and that is sad and lonely and selfish. I didn't know you and I never really thought you'd ever show me YOU. It was some fabrication of what a husband should look like for me and I was always this image of a perfect woman that you created. I was never real and I always compared to fantasy. I am not perfect but at least I own it and wear it like fine diamonds.

You were a snake who slithered and pretended. Happiness was always past tense or instant gratifications for you. I didn't see what others found alluring because eventually your actions wouldn't match your words. You were always conflicted because you could not line those two things up.

I know I matter, but not for arrogant, selfish indulgence. But rather, I matter like sand on a beach. Each grain rubs against and works with all the millions of others to create beautiful shorelines and frothy dunes. I matter because you mattered – we are all the same and equal. Life isn't fair and there are classes and hierarchies. Yet, it is how we treat one another that makes us all work.

You were the one who could give love or withhold it to get your intended result. Your reasons are your own, but the fact was that you kept me at arm's length most of our life together. I miss normal. I miss the life I lived before you.

Even the good and bad. Even the holes and the
challenges. I miss the joy. I want to be free from
you whatever that means. I don't need anything
from you and that was what scared you the most. I
don't need your money or your worries. I feel for
the people who do not truly know you. I pity the
fools who do. I know I am supposed to be, I am, a
better person from knowing you only because you
hurt me, scarred me so deeply. I don't hate you, I
pity you. I love you and always will love you for
giving me Hannah and Dyer. I will never
understand you. Your odd narrative obstructs
your heart, but I know deep in my own heart, that
all my trials and loyalty to you penetrated places
you'd never admit. There was good in you. You
abandoned it with your soul long ago.

Hannah handed the letter to Dyer, her face
stoic. The candy wasn't sweet anymore, the soda
no longer fizzy, the illusion of an infamous
biological father faded as Hannah read her

mother's honest angst. The love Madison and Dyer flung to her so honestly resonated with complete sincerity. For the first time, words on paper had meant the definition of life and death in all the ways that mattered most.

"Your mother would kill me for sharing this letter...but you have to really know he is still a threat." Dyer wanted Hannah to see her mother more honestly.

"He is a monster. I hate how he hurt Mom." Hannah put her face in her hands and sobbed. All the misplaced memories of him made sense. He was more than a bad memory, he was dangerous.

"He turned us all into monsters back then. He'll try to do it again." Dyer put his arms around Hannah and they hugged for a long moment. Hannah's tears pierced the paper note, melting it like bullets through flesh.

Old Love

Things oozed with August. Madison was alone with a very loud silence. The humidity slathered everything in a funk that was slippery, yet elusive. The windows wept tears, begging to come inside before plummeting south. Madison knew her unresolved emotions would only rule her. They would verve out, as in her life before, rather inappropriately and with great resonance only she understood. They ticked loudly, a clock that almost beaconed a sonic, innate attention. That panicky CO_2 she exhaled with her fears often filled the room and stifled the positive oxygen of the true situation. She'd appear the loon, the crazy bird as others she loved watched her go mad. For that is what Rhett Peacock did best – instilled self-doubt to the point his will seemed the only reprieve, the only choice.

Dyer and Madison had turned that paranoia into an accessory worn alongside fine jewelry. They had worn masks of normalcy around their children, masks toward each other. No one felt safe with the knowledge of Rhett's being alive. His sheer essence was weighted. It was beginning, his madness. She could taste blood in the water and that was a familiar palette of the death of so many joys, her former life riddled with murderers and thieves dressed in suits and ties.

Not this time.

It had been a very pensive, distasteful few weeks that everyone begged to relent with the August heat.

Relent - the threat soon would.

The ocean was flat today. It was almost expressionless as if content with hum drum. Madison kicked at the lethargic tide as if to summon a reaction. Nothing. She felt nothingness inside as well. A complacency one might feel with the resolution of death or struggle. She just let go – for once she let life navigate. All the metaphors that surrounded Madison personified themselves with a clarity even a dead woman could recognize.

They began to shine and sing with the subtly of sunrise, the pitch of a choir. It was as if Madison's life was saying BE. How long had it been since Madison had truly experienced the simple touch from joyfulness? Her heart shallow and plastic at times, sporadically unplugged from her emotions. This time Madison just sat down quietly in the sand with her head cradled between her knees and just listened to the still of the waves. A thought washed over her that wasn't her own. *The very thing he wants will be his downfall.* Madison reached for the kite necklace that always hung around her neck. It was a unique kite she had fashioned from all the jewelry Rhett had ever given her. Inside, the hollow necklace housed volumes of information Rhett had stowed away in the elbow of his kite – a kite Madison crashed and broke in her grief years ago. A grief she believed was real. In hindsight, he had planned on stealing what he had stolen during their entire marriage right back from Madison. Madison now knew this was his albatross, not hers. He was taking out everyone around her. It was his style, clear the path to get to the threat. He was coming for her.

A heavy hand imposed Madison's deep digressions. It's gentle purpose instantly recognizable.

"Where are you, Madison?" Dyer whispered softly not to startle her.

"Someplace I should have gone a long, long time ago." Madison mumbled. Her shoulders were winced, postured defensive and rigid, a startled ostrich.

"What does Rhett want?" Dyer sat beside her in the sand, shoulder to shoulder.

"This." Madison showed Dyer the kite necklace. Dyer knew all about it. She never took that necklace off.

"Money and control. Of course." Dyer rubbed her neck, needing to know the stakes for her safety.

The flat waves tried to jump and bob. The tides were pulling at the waves' levity, goading them to dance, find their fierceness.

"He can have it all." Madison's tears rained down from her crystal blue eyes that flickered the flames of her rage.

The tides began to shift and change.

"It's going to be different this time, Madison." Dyer marveled her.

"Really?" Madison looked to Dyer for hope amidst her terror.

"The good guy is going to make sure that the good girl wins." That's why he always knew he'd be with Madison in the end.

He was that good guy she yearned.

Mysterious Gifts

Dearest Family,

How do you explain to rational, grounded folks what works with their perception of safe facts? There are no logical explanations to the strange transmissions of MS? Nerve signals are invisible, their effects mostly unpredictable communications between synapses that fire and spat off like an impulsive child. Controls of the child are only part of the process. Controlling reactions are the key. Emotions are a shifty balance that requires a depth that isn't tethered to the safety of gravity. For I am unfixable, held together by popsicle sticks and duct tape, and frankly, I embrace the anonymity of my invisible disease. MS has always been my mysterious gift. It tied me, pulled me deeper into my truths while the real world tried to "fix" me. Truth - I was never broken. Perception was key. Don't believe everything people say as fact. Don't even believe everything you think because it shackles you in fear and gravity. I am much more than my physicality. I prefer my scarred MS brain, my imperfect fluidity of muddled fingers. They are mine and were given to me to help others.

I was never far from you all those times I seemed absent. Like MS, it was something I had little control over. Only control over how I reacted to it. You always accepted my love in the ways I offered it and you always knew it was unconditional and sincere. That in itself speaks of the faith you have in humanity and the trust you put in your chosen family. I never left you alone – I wasn't far. I know it felt as if my circumstances with MS made it necessary for me to have help or disappear for short periods of time to regroup. I always communicated with you all present or absent. My words were my greatest tool to reach you.

I don't really know how to say this other than to just tell you – I travel through time. I can't put my finger on when these strange burps of time truly began. I think I've always been attuned, just unaware what it was. Like my MS, it was always in my wiring. As with MS, these time warps had a catalyst that sent them into gear. These time warps or mini-vacations from my body had been happening to me since infancy. We are all born with some higher sense, some of us just choose to use it more or less.

It was 1995 when the first significant time travel occurred. That would be the car crash that changed my life forever. All I recalled was swerving and watching a car squeal off the road end over end into a field. I remembered running to the car as best my numb, tingling legs would carry me. It was as if my nervous system became electric with an energy flow of a power grid. I woke up in my beach house attic, back in my teenage body in the 1980's as the morning sun shone through the window seat. I didn't have MS, yet. I felt my present self and my younger self communing. I don't know why, but I ran to my journal and I wrote a letter to myself from 1995. I put down all I recalled as my adult vocabulary began to blend with my teenage lack thereof. I hastily shoved that letter under the boards in my floor, knowing it wouldn't be long before I returned to myself in 1995. I had no memory of what happened after the car crash. They took me to the ER because I had fainted into a bizarre unconsciousness.

I have always had moments of de ja vu my whole childhood and adult life. I was young but never too naïve. An old soul knows things inherently as a child. First things first. Never tell anyone that you traveled in time or left your body. They will commit you. My parents thought I was a crazy child that they had adopted. They feared my DNA for no child talked of future events that wasn't flawed and irrevocable. I think very boldly. I even questioned my own profound revelations, realizing they weren't my human, childlike thoughts such as 'why the sky was blue?' I knew things that most didn't and they could sense that knowing. It often isolated me. I learned to survive by listening to those choice guiding voices. I became a shadow figure in my own life. This viewed curse shaped me, made me a quirky, honest loner of sorts.

I learned this voice was my higher, truest being. It and others were guiding me through the gravity of the human experience. It wasn't rhetoric your insecurities feed or 'to do list' type of monologues rushing like flooding water. It was still, steady and fluid. I guess it is God. It soothed all the mania that my MS physicality had reeked upon me. I never waivered when I allowed myself to rise higher above my frailty and access the big picture. I always fell back into my shell with a gleaning sense of purpose.

No one will truly understand you, but you. I am a total anomaly. We all have our own idiosyncrasies. No one will recognize your mysteries as gifts except you. They will weigh you down like curses when you don't use them. Sickness, illness are just teachers of the still, guiding me to use my powers for good. We all succumb to negative circumstances that challenge *us to grow or just merely move forward. This timelessness had allowed me to view my life for all it's worth. I've been thrown and I've dragged many down dark paths. I've tried to use this current as a way I can soften the edges to some of the very sharp lines I've drawn in my life. I've used some bold markers. Call it selfish, but I've dabbled in erasers for my own heartbeat.*

Like MS, this timelessness had no apparent pattern. It happened at will. Yet, it had always taken me backwards in time. Always landed me in that beach house at different ages of my life. I kept that journal of things to my younger self secret. I hoped that it might improve slightly the trajectory of my life or others'. It felt like magic. I tried to not alter things drastically, just taught myself little bits of maneuvering to make me and others wiser. The last time I disappeared, I went forward. I now know things that I can't share and can't alter.

Lowe had read the letter aloud to her family, perched on the window seat her mother had claimed her third eye; where the girl upstairs, the girl of all ages, spied the sand and the waves, asked and shared with the universe her pains, her joys. She folded the letter back into the same pensive straight edge. She watched everyone connect dots to Gabby's time travel revelations. Lowe had wondered how her mother would return this time. She had been away much more often and for longer periods of time.

Gabby had kept the biggest secret of them all.

Everyone panned the room with a different knowing of the space. It was a sacred spot that had brought them all together, accepting their unique bond as a meant-to-be situation. This letter explained a lot that she hadn't the time to explain to the others. They all embraced in the center of Gabby's room, acknowledged their DNA. They had held all their verbs and adjectives deep in their throats for long enough. Their conversation would be pivotal and hinged on their time traveler's return. Strange winds now blew. It was time to share.

Family Gifts

When you realize you belong, you form bonds of love and commitment. Feelings of caring flow naturally from like people with similar faces or beliefs. Sometimes, belonging occurs with complete strangers. There is some inherent discerning that just clicks. An unlikely family of gifts materializes out of the ties that draw us close or that bind us together. It fates us with a trust we can't fully understand or begin to know. It is faith.

M had laid out all the facts to her family. Back in 1995, the car accident that killed her sister, Madison's mother, had not been an accident at all. The sudden death of Dyer's first wife and Houston King were all, in fact, murders. The morbid photos they had received were not from some detective's case file – the actual murderer took the photos. The murderer had poisoned his victims with a drug that mimicked natural causes. Like the drug Gabby's father had created and was referenced in her letters. M watched their faces connect dots, search memory banks. All the people in Gabby's room knew they were meant to be right there, right now. All knew they were bonded by much more than circumstance or genetics. They had all been brought together through tragedy. They all existed because of unique familial gifts.

M looked around at each beautiful face she had come to cherish. Faces she unknowingly protected at times, others by digging for facts and help from those fallen spirits they had lost. All these faces had a collectiveness, proving that they were far more than bloodlines. They were bonded by their common thread of love. Love that was now being threatened by narcissistic need and control. The one common thread that wove their bits of tragedy - Rhett Peacock.

Traveling Back

Gabby had been gone particularly longer this time and she forged back in time just enough to set a few acts in motion. M had gathered all together and prepared them for this harrowing future event – a display they would all need to understand. This next sequence of future events would not be pretty and best if each were given their role and forewarned. Who played in this game of chess was as important as who did not.

The beach house bedroom had a smell that a blind person could recognize. In Gabby's travel back to the present, she relied on her sense of smell to indicate her location. The olfactory worked for Gabby when her eyes were dim and foggy. Gabby recognized the familiar scent of verbena mixed with suntan lotion – ah, she was in her room once again. Her MS body of the present seized her with ailments. She championed her legs to work, get up and move her. She clunked across the floor sure as if she had wooden legs. She was certain even the neighbors heard her thumping code. Her eyes had readjusted as she surveyed the room. Scattered on the floor were letters and candy wrappers. Empty coke cans signaled a duo, an empty rum drink signaled a trio. Everyone had been waiting for her, holding vigil. For every second seemed like an eternity.

The lock to the door could be heard releasing. Gabby paused, anticipation paralyzed her. It was Madison. In her hands she held all the notes Gabby had left for the girls to read. Somehow the lure of written words had a charm that endeared children, moved them closer to the truth, closer than spoken words from biased parents. The two women shared that loving moment, knowing they were now all aware of their new family. Their faces softened.

"Wow, its really happening just as planned."

"Yes, finally." Gabby crossed her arms.

Madison had been drinking. Gabby could smell the rum across the room.

"I need that rum on your breath." Gabby now understood the empty cocktail glass. Madison had been holding her own court, lying in wait.

Madison stepped on the board in the floor and pulled the small bottle out. She handed it to Gabby.

"Nicely played. You officially know all my secrets." Gabby took a sip of the rum very cautiously.

"I wouldn't say that about any woman." Madison's words were turning cryptic.

"He's coming for us." Gabby cut to it.

"He wants what he believes to be his, those things we hide and protect." Madison's face told a thousand horrible tales in that instant.

"Let's give him what he wants." Gabby offered Madison the rum, selling much more in her wry smile.

"I want something different this time. I want my family." Madison pulled at the chain around her neck that choked her, a noose.

"To find that we are family, that is the gift. What we do with the knowledge defines us." Gabby spoke from a place that had ached for something of her own.

"The moments in time that are coming will define you and connect us forever." Gabby was a player with a plan. Madison looked out the window that the girl upstairs had looked down from for so long. She understood her longing.

"You can't tell me the future, can you? That's how your gift works." Madison looked into the rum bottle, wishing it had the answers.

"Nope. I can't alter it, Madison. The less you know, the better. It will play out in right time." Gabby looked off someplace much further than the room.

"I'm meeting with him tomorrow – here in your room - as planned." Madison reached into the open floorboards and pulled out a small box.

"I believe this is yours." Madison tossed the ornate box to Gabby.

It was dusty and sealed like an Egyptian tomb. Gabby smiled fondly as she examined it.

"It was once priceless to me. I told Rhett it was a family jewel. It housed my keychain necklace from M." Gabby reached for the necklace she never took off and showed it to Madison.

"Give Rhett the empty box. A perfect metaphor." Gabby placed the box back in Madison's palm.

"Give him what he *thinks* he wants." Madison looked panicked and prideful.

"It will give us what we all need." Gabby's eyes jumped all over the room as if she were sizing every inch.

Foreboding

Epic battles are just that – epic and not occurring except every blue eon. Unresolved oozes, the wound that will not and cannot heal. Madison had slept with one eye open, not sure that the silvery moon was protecting her or lighting a path to her. She never took off the necklace or noose, strangely hiding Rhett's secrets as her own.

Rhett Peacock was like picking a scab. He wasn't the sort to feel the compassionate urge to love and protect that she did. He felt the need to pilfer, divide, conquer – which had little to do with emotion and everything to do with calculated motivation. Sociopathic coldness was only understood by those who felt its betrayal and pain. Sociopaths could only feel pain if it had to do with their needs not being met. They took great lust in their own egos being fed and others being squelched. Madison had lived Rhett's emotional tug of war. He reeled her in only enough to belittle her and make her doubt her own worth. He could only do that for so long. Wise women catch on quickly. In order to survive, she had to play his games. It didn't mean she had a way out. Madison had nightmares all those years after Rhett's supposed death. Fearful that some shadow was waiting to snatch her as her family, her children watched, screaming in agony.

Dyer had just pulled up to let Madison out of his truck. The guy in the old beaten up truck looked frail, a former bully. He dangled his make-shift cane out his window and heckled passersby for money. He had possum eyes that stared rigidly and with great intention in their direction, singing and chanting some crazy man tune in his head, yet he focused all too well.

"Wait - I don't like how that man is staring at us." Dyer reached for Madison as she began to open the truck door.

Dyer looked in the direction of the bad vibes. They watched him for a long moment.

"I'll be ok." Madison looked back at Dyer, kissing him on cheek. His chocolate eyes wore worry and anger.

Madison slammed the door shut and began walking in the direction of the building. The old man's vehicle was parked conveniently close to the entrance, his cane pointing in Madison's direction as he grunted and sang uncontrollably. He had a gunshot wound through his chin and his features were grotesque as if he had been burned. The man raised his cane to Madison that was actually a rifle.

"Feeling lucky, pretty girl?" The man spit at Madison.

Madison's ears rushed with her heartbeat, her brain thumped fear. A swift single gunshot pierced the adrenaline of the millisecond. A perfect hole sliced the truck door. Was she dead? Was that why her agony was so raw? Or was it her own unheard shrieks that deafened her sense of space. Madison turned to Dyer whose arm was raised, holding a handgun.

Madison awoke in a cold sweat. She sobbed, putting her face in her pillow to muffle the terror of the dream premonition. Dyer lie awake, the silver shades of the moon highlighted the whites of his open eyes. He heard Madison cry and a single tear poured from his own eye. He didn't have to rouse her and ask her about her nightmare for this time, he had seen it, experienced it simultaneously, but from his point of view.

Madison vs. Rhett

The day was too beautiful for confrontations. It seemed unnatural. The clouds were a soft billowy veil over a crisp blue sky. Birds sang, the waves seemed calm, almost content. It was as if mother nature was soothing and pacifying any self-doubt Madison conjured.

Madison stared out the window, watching for Rhett, knowing she wouldn't see him, she'd hear him. Old habits, old ways never leave, they just lie dormant, always familiar. Her former life with Rhett had quickly become about the unspoken. Cover ups yielded mum unmentionables. Façade masked truths and made the truths appear the monsters. They slayed honesty with unhealthy patterns of fear, discontent, fault. Rhett used disapproval like a weapon. He never hit with his hands, only his words or negative energies.

Old boards never lied. They talked if we listened. Madison heard them creak and her heart began to pound a steady, measured rhythm – her war tempo. The door creaked open and a manicured, male hand appeared first, followed by a shoulder, a thigh, and finally a leg - all dressed in dark brown. A thinning mop of sandy blonde hair was followed by a starry blue eye – eyes Madison saw in Hannah daily. This eye peered with skepticism, sweeping the room. It found Madison's gaze with an almost arrogant relief as if the real threats weren't present. She knew he was trying to disengage her. The wise play along, use their very genuine sincerity to sooth the psychosis manipulating them.

Rhett walked into the room fully and stood sizing Madison up and down. No words were spoken, but things were being said. He looked around the room, listened to the walls. Madison felt certain he heard her steady, ever determined heart beating. He walked closer, taking two steps, as if he were sniffing her out, checking for signs of entrapment. Rhett was a master at absconding and could sniff out lies like fresh baked bread. She watched him and felt very little for him. That she was certain he could sense. He was looking for the old strings attached to her that he could pull one way and get her to do this, the other way and get her to emote that. Madison was string free. She had used his strings as suture for all the wounds he had inflicted in their lifetime together. They were lovely scars that sowed up her seams, shored up her guts. He didn't dare touch her. That would burn him, his repeated betrayals gasoline. He was a calculated animal that found the kindness, the rage, then feasted on it gluttonously. No, Madison wouldn't move, wouldn't speak. She'd let him lead. She didn't dare utter a peep.

"So, how do we do this?" Rhett folded his hands in front of him in a condescending fashion as if he was trying to decide a punishment for their small child.

"Do what?" Madison mirrored his posture. Rhett riddled her with his eyes.

"This." He gestured with his hand – from her to him.

"We don't." Madison cut away the emotional.

"Nothing? You expect me to believe that you feel *nothing*?" Rhett oozed self-righteousness like greasy melted butter, reveled in watching others slip over his words. He was the unfeeling one.

"*This* is what you're selling. I quit buying it long ago." Madison gestured from her to him as he had.

Well, that hadn't worked. Rhett's eyes narrowed as he studied her. Where were her holes?

"This provided you with a good life." Rhett took all the credit for her personal success.

He had always demeaned her abilities in order to mask his inadequacies.

"Nothing good about my life is because of you." Madison crossed her arms. No strings today – ever again.

"Right. You blame me, call me bad...but you walked the same walk. You're just as bad. Trash begets trash." Rhett was tongue whipping her. Madison blinked hard.

"I own my choices." Madison could see sweat beads form on his receding hairline.

"Choices. That is what brings us here again. Those choices." Rhett assumed that tone of inconvenience when he couldn't control somebody. His needs superior.

"I want nothing to do with our collective choices. That is why I am here." Madison could see he didn't like being negated from her life.

"When did you change, have such revelation? We never really change, we morph. How can I believe you aren't the one playing me? I'm not like that simple carpenter." Rhett had thrown the first stone.

"I didn't change. You just never saw the real me. I gave up playing games when I gave up on you." Madison's resolve turned stronger with each jab he doled.

"You can't erase me. What we did together was criminal. You are always tied to me. That's why you are going to GIVE ME EXACTLY WHAT I WANT." Force was what Rhett resorted to when desperation seeped into his ego.

"OR WHAT?" Madison took a step closer to Rhett. Rhett and Madison stood close enough to feel their breaths bounce off the other. It was then, that Rhett spied the kite necklace around Madison's neck. Something became clearer between their stares. Madison bore her telepathy into his dead, calculated eyes. They stated without words.

"OR I'll finish what I started!" Rhett ripped the necklace off her neck. Madison grabbed at her throat, sucking in loud, audible breaths. Freedom from his con. He pushed Madison backwards a few feet.

"NO I will KILL YOU myself before I let you control me ever again." Madison hurled verbal boulders at him, meant to incite.

Rhett shoved the necklace deep into his pocket with one hand and reached into his back pocket and pulled out his pistol with the other. Madison wondered what someone had done, what psychosis riddled him now? What had triggered the switch to flip that sent him to the dark side so recklessly. He was a hollow shell of the man she had once known. His face was crimson, his eyes manic. He pointed the pistol at her and just stared off. He was someplace very threatening.

"Where is the box?" The terroristic telepathy they shared saturated the room with chaotic vibrations.

Madison reached into the desk drawer pulling out the small box. She had taken it from Rhett's safe along with all his secrets after his supposed death. He had stolen the box from Gabby. The box he never forgot that promised fortune. He was merely his compulsions now.

"You mean this little box?" Madison taunted him with his own greed. She knew once she handed the box to him, he would kill her.

"You STOLE that from me." Rhett just stared at the box with a strange fixation she couldn't fathom.

Madison sensed Gabby was in the room.

She felt another heart beating.

It was time to act.

"Nothing in life has ever been YOURS, Rhett Peacock. You've stolen everything. All you do is take – well – now YOU get taken." Madison threw the box at Rhett.

The box bounced, a ping pong ball, off his fumbled efforts to grab it. Madison lunged at his gun as it fired a shot that ricocheted and broke a windowpane. Rhett hit Madison across the face with the handle of the pistol, knocking her backwards and into the window seat, bloodying her cheek.

Rhett's first mistake was scrambling toward his greed and the lithe box that had bounced into the closet. He ripped the curtain back only to find Gabby holding her rightful box.

"Surprise." Gabby swiftly karate chopped his wrist and the gun flung out of his hand, spinning in a Russian roulette fashion as it slid toward the door.

"You're a worthless waste of a woman - give me the box!" Rhett grabbed Gabby by the throat and begun to choke the box out of her grip.

The light above them hummed with Gabby's gurgling desperation.

Dyer flung open the door to Gabby's room as the pistol spun in circles, resting at his simple, work boots. Rhett violently choked Gabby harder.

Dyer recalled the pistol from the dream the night before. He scooped it up with one hand. Madison scampered to Dyer, shaking with hard sobs.

Gabby gave in, dropping the box.

Rhett spun around in his joyous frenzy.

Rhett won again. He had the box.

Dyer had Madison.

Rhett squeezed the box.

Dyer and Rhett locked eyes.

Rhett stared at Madison cleaving to Dyer.

Dyer pointed the gun at Rhett.

Rhett bore his commanding, evil gaze upon Madison.

"You're just a pretty little coward." Rhett crowed a maniacal laugh that had no soul attached to it.

Madison assuredly wrapped her own grip around Dyer's.

"Not today." Madison and Dyer pulled the trigger.

Rhett grabbed his chest arrogantly and with needy drama. His face contorted into all the fear he had instilled. It shimmered like a mirror in his cold blue eyes.

Gabby tugged on this feeble shell of a man and like that, Gabby and Rhett had just disappeared into an ephemeral vapor, time traveling to some future foreign place that would never know that Rhett Peacock had ever existed. This penance worse than death. The room was deafeningly still, only labored breaths bounced off the high walls and the electric pops and snaps from their disappearance. Gabby's lithe box sat, unscathed, in the closet.

Chaotic Comfort

You enjoy
Creating four alarm fires.

You derive strange comfort
In your manipulative chaos.

It camouflages your fears
As someone else's problem.

It shuts people down - numb
Giving you perceived control.

Only distracting, getting
Taking for your needs.

Sad – you only have that fear
Tucking you in each night.

Kindness - that soft place
Between equals.

Vulnerability - your prison
Rather than your free.

April 2017

Woman and the Moon

The strong woman
The admirable foe
Where did she go?

That girl unafraid
Cautiously bent
Down she went?

Down town?
Down stairs?
Who really cares?

Like the moon
Grandiosely bright
Taken for granted in the night.

She shines.

The Marriage of Dyer and Madison

Marriage was a foreign concept for this bride and this groom. Most of their life together was spent in partnership of some sort with death their matchmaker. Madison and Dyer were much better at burying lovers than marrying them. They both tried to protect the innocent or appease the needy and greedy. There wasn't one thing black or white about their love. So this blue sky beach day seemed apropos.

Dyer's work boots clicked rhythmically as he walked around the small cottage he had remodeled with his own hands. A builder by trade for most of his fifty years, he had gotten good at fashioning unique places. Now he had saved his best work for the world he and Madison would create. It was simple and strong just as his intentions for Madison. The old cottage had always talked to him, begged him to rescue its personality from the cookie cutter houses cropping up around it like clever weeds. The gulf beach's lazy, beloved history was being slowly erased by the shimmer of excess.

The cottage was empty, not livable quite yet. He had only the interior to finish out before they could move. Their ten-year-old son, Peck would have to be the new glue that bonded them. Their daughter, Hannah Beth, would graduate from high school in the spring of 2019 and be off to college to glue together her own way.

The sunset ceremony would take place on the long patio steps of the cottage and a small reception would be held in their raw, unfinished home. Bare white light bulbs hung on strings from an open ceiling giving the illusion of a sky full of stars. One table sat in the middle of the room with jars of colorful shells and pictures of their patchwork quilt of a family that life had chosen for them. Another table sat in the corner and housed the cake, seafood, and cocktails. The food and drink was for the small gathering of family. Afterwards, Dyer and Madison were going to walk the beach with their kids, build a fire, and cook s'mores.

Today felt quiet, reverent. Simple permeated the seams of the occasion. The hum of energy could be felt as the old and new friends gathered and chatter blended like the banter of the ocean waves. The smell of cooked seafood grew with the shifting sun.

Dyer wore khakis, a white button down shirt, and work boots. He stood with his hands in his pockets just soaking up the spirit of the moment. Music piped robustly through the surround sound system Dyer had prided himself on installing just for today. Gerry Rafferty sang "It's been you, woman, right down the line." Madison walked through the door. She wore a white blouse, khaki capris, and sandals. Her dark hair was cut in a bob that fell forward slightly with the tilt of her head and widening of her eyes and smile.

Madison reached for Dyer, wiggling her bony fingers. It was time. A flutter of butterflies raced Dyer's spine, landing in his stomach. They stared at one another across the room for a long second before Dyer joined Madison. Dyer wrapped his strong, calloused fingers into Madison's firm grip, kissing her knuckles as the light bulbs flickered in karmic unison. They opened their door, walked their deck, stood on steps they had built to a beautifully tangled life.

Madison's aunt and justice of the peace, M, was performing the marriage. She watched them navigate the stairs towards her, her more salt than pepper hair creating a halo effect for her piercing blue eyes that mirrored the sky. Wonderful eyes of wisdom and kindness that had manifested after a twenty-year tragedy. Eyes that had finally cut through Madison's skin and bones straight to her heart.

Hannah proudly joined her mother's side. Hardly the little lost girl with starry blue eyes and blonde pigtails looking for a mother, but rather a confident young girl in a blossoming woman's body. Madison's niece, Lowe, shared this space beside Hannah – another daughter friend – a lovely mentor and guide for Hannah and Peck. Peck followed the girls' lead and joined Dyer's right side. Peck was tall for ten. Dyer fist-bumped Peck and just smiled at this boy man he had adopted as his own.

Small crowds of family and friends stood behind M on the beach. As the sun sank, the guests grew tall, skinny shadows in the fading light. The shadow auras of those lost multiplied and contrasted the small group.

Madison found her gaze pulled down a few houses toward Gabby's infamous window. She had been thinking of her sister friend today. She wondered where time had been taking her. Dyer watched Madison's distraction with skill, smiling at her. As Dyer and Madison were pronounced husband and wife, their congruent patchwork family of different last names, became simply and officially the Browns.

Everywhere and Nowhere

The beach in April was stunning. It wasn't too hot yet, still blue skies and a breeze. Friends had begun to gather, the weather beckoning community. Beach goers moved like ants, filing out to build a place to nest. It was reminiscent of that collective childhood. Everyone needs a beach. There is something about it that is a second home to most. Quite possibly because we feel akin to the rhythm of the waves, the safety and comfort of the still it provides us within. It keeps our secrets, grounds our gypsy natures. It settles old scores, washes away our fears, catches our dreams and returns them with high tide. The beach reminds us of who we once were, who we are, and who we can become. We are all merely beach goer ants in life's grand tapestry, each with their job.

Gabby stood staring out the window at the April morning. For her, a beach was a state of mind. No matter what far off place she found herself, she could always feel at home in its comfort. She took it with her wherever she journeyed and accessed it when she needed it most. When she yearned for it, it delivered and sent her back to it, over and over, reminding her of its safety, its magic.

For Gabby and her family, the last year and a half had been about exhaling. No one died. No one threatened or rebelled. It was a time of healing and acceptance, swallowing some hard earned truths. Gabby assumed her throne, her window seat view, forever the girl upstairs. She noticed her own heart beating in the room. It was her baby, her space she created, a space she now shared.

This beautiful canvas of art unfolding out the window before her eyes, was this moment real? Was this reality or a memory? Lovely fruit from her labors of love? She hadn't returned to this space since that fateful eradication of Rhett. That day she used her gifts for Rhett Peacock one final time. Where in the future she had ended up she wasn't certain. She only knew that she had left Rhett in his personal purgatory; a place where he was nobody.

Where Gabby's gift took her afterwards was a blur. It was the closest thing to heaven she could imagine, and yet there were no spirits that she knew. It allowed Gabby to view her time travel with all the small, inconsequential tweaks as a collective whole. It whispered to her, imparted a story, the story, the fabric she created with those simple wrinkles, choices in time. The stellar story she now viewed from her window.

With every interruption, every suffering, her own MS had given her, it had also given her powerful gifts to transform and shape others. Gabby was able to edit and line up the correct story for her family's future. She chose the good. Gabby lived with an urgent unpredictability all her life, but it was what she did with it that made her scattered existence matter. Ultimately, no one controlled her or those she loved. Gabby was the master storyteller in her own life and the lives she wove together with love. She would teach others that we are all swatches of fabric from a universal tapestry. We are all everywhere and nowhere sometime in our journey.

I Need a Beach

I need an ocean
Give me a sea.
Wrap me in devotion
Throw away the key.

Silence your chatter
Your verbal barrage.
You do matter
Practice humble assuage.

I need that beach
To validate my soul
Lend emotional reach
Within my control.

Weary won't weep
They persevere
They tend to the sheep
Never balk fear.

Arrogance with blindness
Just selfish need.
Give an ocean of kindness
Let love lead.

Author Epilogue

by

Monica C. Petter

My perspective and great love of the gift of illness is the driving force throughout all I write. My MS wisdom is as much or more my third eye narrating to you these character's stories. I've had MS since I was twenty. The storms in the distance for me are always MS. What is your storm? How would you navigate your storm, embrace it to find your truth? How you share your storm is even more important than surviving it. This book was written from those inspired spaces of trial.

I had never considered my first two novels a series or a set. *Kite Strings* and *The Girl Upstairs* were mutually exclusive moments in time for the characters in their respective lives. It just happened that in the second book, *The Girl Upstairs*, the characters showed their connectedness by crossing Madison Peacock into Gabrielle Vansant's life. You could read the books in any order and they stood alone. They were their own plights. You could call them cousins, not siblings.

When I first started writing *Everywhere and Nowhere* back in 2016, it was meant to show the growth of the characters from my first novel *Kite Strings*. It quickly became apparent that this book would combine that connectedness with characters from both the other novels. There was a shared resolution necessary in the two lead female characters that made it impossible not to weave these characters into a final shared tapestry. Like those two characters, Gabby and Madison, I shared a similar need for resolution in my own life that I would only gain by writing *Everywhere and Nowhere* from that connectedness. The three novels work together with a synergy that is beautifully threaded. We are all connected by that in-between. That space where we connect with the love made while we lived, shared when we die, making us forever, *Everywhere and Nowhere*.

My Gifted Disease

Sickness has distance around it, circumference.
It creates invisible gloves
Doubt in how to handle a lack of control
Unforeseen strings now puppet the journey.

Illness casts a long profile
When the good light is involved
Mimics our truest actions
Exposes our fable faces.

Malady is that teacher
That frightens with depths of knowledge
Intrigues with fleeting light
And changes how we reach for others.

Disease is my monocle.
My compass to my little bits of God
That steer, magnify my sincerity.

I don't plug into the hum and chatter
Of societal busy bees that float flowers.
Power is an egoistic lush.
I find heart a more copious goal.

Logic has its fleshy limits
Disorder is that phantom never understood
It defies eyes with empathy
THE universal truth – it is a gift.

Monica C. Petter is a poet, author, photographer – artist.

Monica is a native of Stuttgart, AR. She has 9 books of poetry and prose. She was a poet laureate nominee for the state of Arkansas. Her childhood pencil sketches turned to teenage poetry. Her adult poetry matured to prose. Her art found photography and then painting. Art always found a way through and out of her.

Monica was diagnosed with Multiple Sclerosis at the age of twenty. She considers disease to be her greatest teacher and most benevolent gift. Her perspective the key.

Monica's Other Novels:
Kite Stings
The Girl Upstairs